CROSSIN
OVER

New writing for a new South Africa

Compiled by Linda Rode
with the assistance of Jakes Gerwel

Kwela
B·O·O·K·S

A detail from "Unification", a linocut
by Vuyisani Mgijima,
appears on the cover with the kind permission of
the South African National Gallery in Cape Town.

Contents

Acknowledgements

An earlier version of "Two fishermen" by Jenny Hobbs appeared in *Contrast* in September 1975;
"Red sports car" was adapted by Michael Williams from his novel *Crocodile burning*, published by Loadstar Books, New York, in 1993.

Stories originally written in Afrikaans were translated by Pieter Bezuidenhout, Mary Hayter, Lindsay King, Catherine Knox and Chris van Wyk.

This collection is also available in Afrikaans under the title *Keerpunt*.

Foreword

South African society has made a remarkable transition. This transition, marked most spectacularly by the success of the inclusive, non-racial elections of April 1994 and the inauguration of the first democratically elected and universally respected president, has grabbed the imagination. This collection of stories bears the stamp of that transition.

The inspiring coming together of a divided nation during and immediately after the April elections, signalled the crossing of a divide which had liberating effects far beyond the obviously political: the awakening of an awareness of others, a loosening of the paralysing bonds of fear and suspicion, the dawning sense of self, the possibility of remembering and speaking about pain without unleashing destruction, the emancipation of the personal from the overbearing domination of the political.

This volume is the product of an invitation to writers to contribute stories dealing with some kind of crossing over. Contributors were required (in their stories to) give insight into the world of young people entering adulthood amidst the wide-ranging changes in South Africa today. It was hoped that a rounded picture of our times and society would emerge from the variety of contributions received, and that the collection would give readers from different backgrounds – be it cultural, linguistic, geographical, economic or religious – a window on the worlds of others.

Every effort was made to involve as representative a group of South African writers as possible. Well-known as well as lesser known and previously unpublished writers were invited; fiction writers as well as journalists and dramatists; authors associated with writing for adults and writers associated with a teenage readership; senior as well as younger writers; women and men; city dwellers as well as people living in rural areas.

Writers were invited to submit contributions in any of the South African languages, with contributions not in English to be translated for this first publication of the collection. The intentions with this project were that, depending on the response from libraries, educationalists, and others, the collection would be made available in one or more of the other South African languages as well. An Afrikaans edition is presently in preparation. It is worthy of note and cause for reflection that in the end all contributions were either in English or Afrikaans.

If the eventual crop is still not representative of all the social sectors of our society, in each of which there must certainly reside a wealth of talent and creativity waiting to be unearthed and released, it points to the suffocating burden of our history. At the same time, it challenges writing and reading in this country to play its part in the process of healing required for the miracle of our transition to become a permanent reality. This collection hopefully contributes in some significant way to our talking with one another in new keys, and talking about ourselves with new freedom and openness.

Jakes Gerwel
Cape Town
March 1995

Michael Williams

Red sports car

The smell of sour milk is strong in the kitchen. I put the tip of my thumb over the wriggling fly and slowly press down. This is another reason I'm angry with my mother. She knows about Mr Nzule's women, but she does nothing about it. She allows him to bring women here when she's at work, and then pretends not to notice the smell they leave behind.

If I move now, I can be out the back window without their knowing that I've seen them. They're almost at the door. I can hear her laughter. If I stay, Mr Nzule's smile will turn into a frown when he opens the door, and then to a scowl, as I stare him and his woman down.

I shove my chair back noisily, on purpose, push the table aside, and slip out through the back window. I dash across the yard and run down the alley out into the street. It is crowded with people just off the 3:15 train from the city. They move down the road like peas rolling out of a can. The mini-buses are lined up, raring to go, and the drivers shout their destinations as the crowd moves toward them. People shout back and haggle with the drivers. Struggling with their shopping parcels, ten, twelve, maybe even fourteen, get into one of the many mini-buses, which speed away to all the zones in the township.

I stop running, and wait at the side of the road for a Pick 'n Pay truck, which is weaving its way slowly through the hurrying people. It is easy to scramble up to the foothold on its back bumper, and to hold on to the lock of its doors. I like being above the crowd, feeling the wind in my face, and moving with the truck as it picks up speed. The swirling dust of the open road pricks my eyes, but I shout over the roar of the truck's engine as the speed lifts me and carries me away from home. Home. Suddenly, I want to let go and fall back to the ground. I want to be tossed and bruised and feel the cut of the stones and broken bottles that litter the roadway as I hit the earth. I wish I had money, lots of money. I wish I were far away, beyond everything: naked, skinned and dead. I wish . . .

"Hey, you! Get off there!"

I turn my head to the side and blink the dust from my eyes. A shiny red sports car has come up behind my truck. A fat man is leaning his head out the window and shouting at me. The driver's blowing the hooter. The fat man shouts again.

"Get off there! You'll kill yourself!"

The car pulls up alongside me. I stare at it, pretending not to understand what the man is shouting.

"Hey, did you hear? Get off!"

The car moves ahead. The driver shrugs and waves at me. His companion rolls up his window, shaking his head. The car's exactly the kind of red I like – fire-engine red! I edge along the back of the truck, stretching around its corner to peer after my red sports car, as if moves off into the distance.

Then the truck's wheel beneath me jolts into a deep rut, and my foot jumps free and drags on the rushing ground. I cling desperately to the lock and pull myself back up onto the truck and tighten my grip. Sweat burns my eyes and trickles down my neck. The truck's moving too fast now. I look for a way off, but cars are running too close behind, and beside the road there's only a blur of dusty, hard ground and gravel.

A van is trying to overtake us. Its driver keeps his hand on the hooter, and my truck slows down to let him pass. Now's my chance.

I jump, hit the ground, stumble, and fall free of the traffic. I lie gasping for air to fill my chest, and slowly feel pain in many places. I've scraped and torn my arm, cut my leg, and my head is swimming. I stagger to my feet and force myself to focus on the image of a red sports car. I shake my head and rub the haze from my eyes. I can't believe what I see. There, in front of me, stands the shiny red sports car. Just as I had imagined. It is the bold, fancy red I like, and it has the same fat wheels and silver hubcaps that I dreamed of. Except now it's parked outside a battered old building instead of in my driveway. Checking the traffic, I limp across the road to get a closer look.

Some kids are gawking at their reflections in the gleaming bonnet. I push past them as I move slowly around my car. A pair of driving gloves is lying on the leather bucket seat on the right. Other boys are stroking the handles, smearing their snotty noses on the windows, and making the sound of an engine roaring. I want to push them

2

away, tell them not to touch my car. Instead, I stand apart and watch them mess all over this red wonder which sped past me.

Behind me, people are going into the building. It looks like some sort of community centre. I recognise a popular tune coming from the open door. I move to just inside the doorway. Everyone's talking and laughing, and several people are standing around a piano. There is too much of a crowd for me. I am turning to leave when a hand on my shoulder stops me.

"So you managed to get off that truck without too much loss of blood?"

This is not the fat man who yelled at me, so it must be the driver. He speaks in a low, gravelly voice, as if his words come from somewhere deep in his chest. He's taller than I am, and he grips my shoulder hard. I can feel the strength in his fingers. I mumble and shake off his hand. Nobody touches me.

"You've come for my audition?" He is smiling, but I notice that his eyes are not. It's a thin smile for such a wide mouth, and it doesn't seem to fit among the solid features of his face.

"Is that your car?"

"Yes. Smooth, isn't it?"

"Fire-engine red."

"You're auditioning?" he asks again. I don't really know what he's talking about, but it sounds like a challenge.

"Yes," I say.

"Good. Go to the toilet and clean up. We're starting now."

"Mosake, you can't be serious. Not that terrorist!"

It is the passenger in the sports car. I feel like punching him in his big fat face. His shirt is bright orange, and his belly bulges out between the buttons and hangs over his belt.

I go into the toilet and look around. There is an open window and empty yard outside. I could get out through this window easily. I don't have to stay. I look in the mirror. My face seems small compared with Mosake's. I have thin lips, a broad nose, a scab on my forehead from last week's street fight, and small eyes. I don't belong here. I could climb through this window, run across the yard, and be gone. Nobody would miss me. I stand on the toilet seat, push the window open.

Then I hear the piano again in the other room. This time there is singing. It's loud and it's a tune I don't know. I step down from the toilet and listen with my ear to the door.

3

It is the sound of an open veld, of clouds racing across the sky, and of the wind chasing through long grass. The girls' voices rise high above the boys', and then the melody changes and the singers begin clapping and stamping. Now the sound is of a Friday afternoon at the train station: hooting, shouting, hurrying feet and wailing sirens. These are songs I don't know, but the music is familiar and it gets to me and I like what I hear.

I consider the open window again. I would run past the red sports car, disappear into the streets. I could run. I could. But then I hurry to wash the dust from my face and clean up my arm. There is no reason not to stay and listen to the music. This window will be here later.

The main room is now full of boys and girls standing nervously around the piano, or singing in a small group in the centre of the floor. The walls are lined with parents who sit on battered chairs. I think of Mr Nzule and his woman, my mother and her work.

At the far end of the room Mosake is sitting with his hands loosely clasped on the table before him. He's watching the singers closely. Even right at the end of the room he is at the centre of everyone's attention. Everyone is singing for him. He watches, without smiling or frowning; he doesn't seem to know that he is at the centre. For some time he studies the singers without moving, and then his head turns and his gaze shifts sideways and falls on me.

We stare at each other. I'm not afraid of him. I didn't climb out the window. He drives my car.

He points at me and then at the singers in the centre of the room. I nod and walk over to the group, who move apart to allow me among them. The fat pig sucks on his pencil, jots something down, and murmurs to Mosake. I ignore them and start singing.

It's easier than I'd expected; the other singers cover my mistakes. I become part of the sound of a Friday afternoon, and feel my voice disappear into the other voices, feel my head fill with notes I've never sung before. Soon I begin to hear my own sound among the others and am surprised that although I sing with them, my voice sounds separate.

We're told to sing the first song again, and now I sing louder, hearing the melody of the open veld, racing with the wind through tall grass, riding the white clouds, and adding my own harmony.

"That's enough," Mosake says, and stands up.

4

Everyone stops singing.

"Now dance for me!"

No one moves, except to glance at one another.

"Come on. Dancing is part of this."

Behind me, a boy and a girl giggle nervously. Our feet seem nailed to the floor. The boys look helplessly down at their shoes. The girls stare blankly at Mosake. Someone at the back asks if we couldn't have some music to dance to.

"Later you'll have music," he says. "Now I want to see what kind of young people I have before me. Dance to your own music."

I think of the open window. The red sports car. Mr Nzule and his women. My mother. I begin to sway from side to side, softly chanting a song I know:

> The sorrow that is Soweto
> Dark clouds gather over you
> When will the rains come
> To wash our sorrow away?

I shift my feet and dance alone – until another boy joins me and we sing and dance together. We lift our voices and grow stronger, and when I raise my fist above my head, a third and then a fourth boy picks up our beat, and then all of us are moving from side to side, singing, stamping our feet, and filling the room with our voices. I feel my anger turn to joy as we chant and bounce to the rhythm of the toyi-toyi. One foot up, the other a hop, down again, up again, one foot up, the other a hop, down again, up again –

"Stop!"

Everyone goes tense around me. In silence we wait while Mosake talks to the fat man. Then he jabs his finger at a short girl in front – "Out!" – and one of the boys standing beside me – "You, next to the terrorist! Out!"

The girl moves to the side where her mother puts her arms around her and leads her toward the door. The boy mutters a curse and then walks proudly out of the room alone. Everyone else is shuffling about, trying not to be at the end of Mosake's finger.

"What is he doing?" I whisper to the boy next to me.

"Shhh, it could be you next."

We go on. Dancing and singing.

"You, out," Mosake's finger points again. "And you, too. You may leave now."

It is getting later, and there are only twenty of us left, as Mosake sits at his table, cold, aloof, watching, instructing, and never changing his expression or his tone of voice.

"You, out! And you! Out!"

I like the power Mosake has. It's swift and fierce. He only has to point his finger. He will not point his finger at me. I did not climb through that window, and now with only eighteen of us left, I feel like I'm clinging to that high-speed truck again. Only this time it's not a truck and I'm not worried about how to get off. This time I'm loving the thrill and the danger of holding on, of not knowing where I'm going.

Slowly, Mosake rises, stretches, and walks to the front of his table. For a big man he moves gracefully, without ever seeming hurried. He leans lightly against the table, folds his arms, and nods as if he is thinking something of great importance. His face shows no emotion, yet his dark eyes draw us to him. When he speaks it is as if he's talking to each one of us alone.

"Right, that's it. You eighteen have been chosen. You are what I want."

Some of the boys shout, some of the girls shriek with excitement, two boys slap hands with each other, girls are hugging one another. I do nothing. What does he mean that we are chosen?

"We start rehearsals next Monday," Mosake begins. "We'll work every afternoon during the week and all day Saturdays. No one is to use this production as an excuse to miss school," he adds, looking straight at me. "You'll be paid seven rand a rehearsal and ten rand a performance. The performances will be held at the new community centre."

Seven rand a rehearsal and ten rand a performance! We're to be paid for dancing and singing? It's crazy! I'm going to be paid money for doing the *toyi-toyi*! Mr Nzule will never believe me. He'll say I stole the money. Seven rand a rehearsal and ten rand a performance! It's a fortune!

Mosake turns his back to us and begins to gather up his papers from the table. As he opens his briefcase he says, "You understand that I expect perfect attendance and one hundred per cent effort at all times. Anyone who thinks he can get away with giving less had better leave now." He continues to pack his case.

6

Nobody moves. The room is silent except for the rustling of his papers.

"Good! Then we are all in agreement. I will see you all on Monday straight after school. My rehearsals start promptly. Don't be late." He turns, looks us over one last time, and leaves the room. His fat friend takes his pencil from his mouth, twists it around, and then puts it behind his ear. He scratches his enormous belly and burps. He looks at us doubtfully, shakes his head, and follows Mosake to the door.

The boy standing next to me says, "Well, welcome aboard. It can be a bumpy ride in places, but that's showbiz. You're on your way to the moon. See you on Monday," and then he runs out the hall.

I don't know what he's talking about. Mosake is gone and somehow the room looks ordinary, as if nothing important has happened here. Whatever it was, it is over. Everyone has left.

I go to the door and look outside. The adults are standing near their cars calling to their children. The world outside this room looks ordinary too. Nothing's changed. The evening cooking fires have been lit, and the haze of smoke is beginning to collect over the township, dimming the street lamps and the lights of cars. The roads are busy with commuters from the city, carrying their weekly pay packets, their feet stirring up the dust. The Naughty Boys and the shebeen queens are out there, too, waiting to get their share of other people's money. It's Friday night just like any other Friday night, but for me it's different.

Today I followed a red sports car.

And I sang.

Michael Williams was born in Pretoria and grew up in Cape Town. He has been a teacher in Kathmandu, Nepal, an assistant producer for New Sadler's Wells Opera in London and a drama lecturer on board ship for the University of Pittsburgh's Semester at Sea programme. He is currently a Staff Director for the CAPAB opera department at the Nico Theatre in Cape Town. He has written four operas for young people, among others, *The orphans of Qumbu*, and more recently the libretto for *Enoch, Prophet of God*. The author's books for young adults include *My father and I, Into the valley, Crocodile burning, The genuine half-moon kid* (awarded the 1992 Sanlam Gold Prize for Youth Literature) and *Virgin twins*.

Jenny Hobbs

Two fishermen

It's no fun swimming alone, Helen thought, as she plunged under a wave, the water seething past her ears. She wanted to come up wide-eyed and laughing as those girls did in shampoo and cigarette ads, with little drops of sea water sparkling on her eyelashes. But her only audience would have been her father, and he was lying far up the empty beach with his head in the shade of a fringed umbrella.

She came up in the smooth swell behind the wave, blinking through a heavy wet net of hair, and feeling the sand under her feet, pushed herself off in front of the next wave, surfing with it until it curled over hissing and slid her up the glittering slope of the beach. After it had receded she lay with her head on her arm watching the slick wetness sink away into the sand, and the pink sand crabs scuttling down to the water's edge and then dancing back in comical sideways jerks before the next wave could catch them.

There were pockets of coarse-grained sand in her bra when she got up. She brushed them out and walked towards the umbrella. Her father had moved entirely into its shade and was sitting on his towel reading a paperback.

"Have a good swim?" He put down the book, his eyes half closed behind the dark lenses.

"Mmm. Water's quite cold today."

Out of the corner of her eye she saw him frown. I know just what he's thinking, she thought – Helen's lonely.

Her parents had always disliked holidays spent in hotels. They had built the cottage in the south coast bush themselves, adding haphazard rooms as the family grew. But now her sisters were married, and she was the only one left.

She thought, it's their predictability that makes parents so boring. You always know what they're thinking and how they'll react.

She put on a careful smile and said, "Come on, Pa, let's go up for lunch. I'm starving."

He looked relieved, and got up with one hand on his knee to dismantle the umbrella. Now it's all right, she thought, because it's expected that I'd be starving after a swim, at my age.

They toiled up the path. The walls of the cottage were blurred by many layers of whitewash and there were rain tanks at each corner. It lay behind the first row of dunes on a patch of threadbare lawn hollowed out of the bush. A row of salt-bleared windows looked out through the sprawling branches of a milkwood tree and along the curve of the bay to the rocky point where the fishermen came on holidays and at weekends with their kites and heavy tackle, after game fish.

After lunch, her mother asked the usual question: "Resting, dear?"

Her parents always rested on their beds and read books until tea-time. The afternoons were close and sticky, cicadas shrieked in the bush and the hot beach sand burned tender bare feet. It was a pleasant feeling to lie with a slack salty body and sandy legs on a cool sheet, reading.

But she said, "No, I think I'll walk along to the rocks at the point."

"Won't it be too hot?"

"Can't I go for a walk if I want to?" Her voice was suddenly loud. "I'll make sure I don't get heatstroke or anything."

Her mother turned without a word and walked into the bedroom, closing the door with a precise click. And Helen stamped down to the beach forgetting both her floppy hat and her sandals so that she had to run with burning feet across the sand to the foamy edge of the waves. The bright restless sea-dazzle made her eyes water and the gusting breeze blew her hair into them. All the way along the beach she was furious with herself for being so predictable.

At the point there was a steady wind blowing. Four kites were up, red and yellow diamonds against the blue sky. If you searched the choppy water between kites and fishermen you could see their markers, fluttering white rags tied to the line above plastic bottle floats.

Helen climbed up on to a rock. There wasn't much else to do once you reached the point but watch the fishermen. She had to justify the long uncomfortable walk. Perhaps one of them would catch a shark or even a barracuda, and she would watch it arcing its steel blue torpedo body against the sand as it was gaffed and dragged in triumph from the sea.

Two Indian men stood with one of the stubby kite rods, taking turns at keeping it seated in leather rod buckets strapped round their waists, gloved hands on the big wooden reel. A woman sat near them in the partial shelter of a low rock, with a curry-streaked aluminium pot and a bowl bound in a white cloth at her feet. She had pulled the end of her sari over her mouth against the wind and sat huddled patiently, unspeaking, undemanding.

Not far away, Kenny Harper was fishing with his father and another white man, all three of them watching their markers with eyes screwed small against the blowing spray and the glare, cigarettes smoking in their cupped hands. Now and then one would lift his arm and pull with hollowed cheeks at his cigarette, which glowed briefly as the wind tore away the ash.

She wondered if Kenny would turn round and see her. They were the same age and had often played together on the beach as children, their peeling noses bent side by side over rock pools. She remembered how they had used pebbles to smash open the tough, discoloured oysters at low tide, looking for pearls. And how they had spent one whole morning sticking their fingers into the soft open rosettes of every sea anemone they could find, just to feel the eerie suck of closing tentacles. But there came a summer when Kenny had begun to go fishing with his father every day, and their friendship had dwindled to an awkwardly mumbled "Hullo" when they met on the beach.

Beyond the Harpers, where the rocks fell away to the curving beach of the next bay, she watched a black fisherman casting in the surf for shad. Again and again he swung his rod back, legs braced, and with a muscular flick of his arms sent the silvered spoon flashing far out over the breakers before it plummeted into the sea. Each time the spoon dragged back with empty hooks. Presently he fastened it under his reel, picked up a khaki canvas fishing bag and started to trudge into the wind, heading towards the place where Helen sat on her rock. His shadow undulated over the rows of footprints along the beach. Unwincing, the bare feet trod through sunbaked sand that would have burned Helen's soles raw after twenty steps.

When he came closer, she saw with some surprise that he was young, perhaps twenty-five. He wore an old white shirt and patched jeans rolled up over sinewy calves. Under the brim of a salt-stained felt hat, his dark brown face was lean and smooth with high cheekbones and a prominently curved, almost Arabic, nose.

Is he the descendant of a slave trader? she wondered, and imagined shadowy dhows running before the wind and a proud Arab captain watching a beaded Zulu maiden walk past, gracefully balancing a water pot on her head. She'd be the decoy, of course, while her brothers hid trembling in the bush. He would love and leave her and later there'd be a son whose face would bear an arrogant desert beak, fit for a hawk . . .

She was staring at the fisherman as he neared her rock, rapt in her fantasy, when he slowed down to get a better grip on his rod and lifting his head, looked directly at her.

Unable to look away quickly enough, Helen blushed and reacted with a tentative smile. The fisherman stumbled and stopped.

There was a lull in the wind. She felt the intensified heat of the sun burning her arms, and the roughness of the granite rock thrusting up under her feet.

After a moment he nodded curtly and dropped his eyes to resume his trudging walk before the smile could die on her face.

When he was out of sight, Helen jumped down and started to walk slowly home along the water's edge, burying her feet ankle deep at each step in the fine wet sand so that they left a chain of little round seeping pools behind her. She could not stop thinking about the fisherman's reaction. Instead of dissolving into the usual ingratiating smile, his full lips had firmed together as he nodded. He had not touched his hat or murmured a polite greeting as older black men would have done.

Back at the cottage she said nothing about the incident, knowing what her parents' reaction would have been: no more solitary walks.

And she liked being alone on the beach, walking and thinking. After the first few days she managed to discourage her father from his dutiful efforts to keep her company. Her days were governed by the changing tides and the veering winds that blew often during the summer. South-easters would bring drizzling rain, and with the north-easters would come flotillas of stinging bluebottles, which meant no swimming.

For several days she looked out for the black fisherman during her walks, but did not see him. There had been rain inland, the sea was rough and stained with river mud, and the fishing was poor. After a while she began to wonder whether she had not imagined the assessing look on his face.

Next time she walked to the point, she took off her watch to plunge her arm into one of the rock pools, reaching for a tiny white pearl of a cowrie whose form was as perfect as its name, "angel's tear". Turning it over and over in her hand, she quite forgot her watch.

When she went back to look for it the following morning, it was gone.

Her father was unwilling to work up the proper degree of annoyance on his holiday. He said in mild reproach, "Dozens of people traipse over those rocks every day, Helen. Anyone could have found it. You'll just have to do without until your birthday."

She couldn't bear to go to the point again after that, but went in the opposite direction to the lagoon at the river mouth, to lie on the sand bank and watch the grey mullet shadows slipping through the muddy shallows. No one swam at the river mouth because of sharks, but on the way there and back would be family groups with picnic baskets under flapping umbrellas, and occasional fishermen, and kids messing around in rock pools with their buckets.

One afternoon, coming back from the lagoon, she saw a man approaching far along the beach and as he came closer, recognised him by the old felt hat.

With a faint sense of alarm she saw him quicken his pace as he caught sight of her. It was an unpleasant windy day and the only people on the beach had been a couple of hardy swimmers.

She looked for the path to the cottage and saw it only a beach-width away, close enough for escape if she hurried. Vague pictures of being dragged behind a lonely dune and raped flickered like a silent movie through her mind. What shall I do? she thought, and stood hesitating with her hair whipping across her eyes. Behind her, planing into the wind, a gull suddenly screamed.

She began to run. When she reached the sheltered stillness of the path and looked back through the archway of cut-back amatungulu bushes, she saw the black fisherman standing by the sea with his face raised to watch her retreat. He made no move to follow her. When she looked again, he was gone.

There was a gale in the night and the next day it was still blowing. Wet branches brushed against the windows of the cottage, making it dank and gloomy. There was nothing to do but read.

At five her father said, slapping his book energetically down, "It's stopped raining. Let's all go for a walk to blow the cobwebs away."

Almost carried along by the furious wind, the three of them walked to the point and turned round to struggle home again. The sea roared and gnashed at the beach, each wave a fury of salt spray. It was an effort to shout above the wind.

Helen began to enjoy herself. After the long, dull day indoors it felt good to be out in the open, battling the elements. Busy searching through newly dumped piles of debris for shells, she dropped behind, wanting as usual to be alone but glad of the well-wrapped bulky figures of her parents plodding ahead of her.

Just as they reached the entrance to the path, she saw the fisherman again, sitting on one of the dunes, his delivery-man's khaki plastic rain cape inconspicuous against the wet greens of the bush. He was watching her, holding something in his hand.

This time he made no move towards her, but she thought he turned his head to look pointedly at her parents and then back again at her.

She wavered as before, gripped by a strong feeling that it was cowardly to run away. But the panicky thought that he had taken her initial smile for encouragement flashed again through her mind. Now she was really afraid. It's not only that he's black either, she told herself. He's a grown man, after all.

She turned and fled after her parents, hurrying with a thumping heart up the winding path to the stuffy lamplit sanctuary of the cottage. And resolved not to walk on the beach alone for the rest of the holiday.

The storm blew itself out during the night and the next day the sun began to shine again from a clear blue sky. She hung about the cottage, self-consciously paging through the pile of required reading in her suitcase, or just lying on the lawn in the sun. Her behaviour was so docile that her mother asked several times if she felt unwell.

"Oh Ma, of course not! I just thought I'd better get through these books because there'll be so little time when we get home."

"In other words, you're bored."

"I didn't say so."

"You don't have to. I think perhaps this holiday was a mistake," her mother said. "You've been alone too much. I wish we had asked one of your friends down."

"I'm quite happy on my own, really." And she had been, until the last few days' unease over the fisherman.

Her mother said suddenly, "I know, I'll ask the Harpers and Kenny over to supper tomorrow. Pa said he saw them on the beach."

"Oh please don't, not for my sake. It'd be too embarrassing. Kenny's not remotely interested in me any more, and I – " Helen trailed off, seeing the pleased deaf look that was settling on her mother's face.

Next day when the Harpers came, she put on a pretty pink cotton dress despite her irritation at being organised, and was surprised and pleased to find Kenny quite friendly towards her. He talked all through the meal about his intention to study engineering and the thrill of catching a big game fish. At the end of the meal Helen allowed her mother to shoo them off to the beach with scarcely a murmur of protest.

It was strange to have a tall Kenny with solid hairy legs walking beside her, when she remembered him as a skinny boy. He looked down and caught her sideways glance. Grinning, he said, "You've grown into quite a girl, Helen."

She slid her eyes away and could not help blushing. What did one say? "Thanks."

"*Quite* a girl. Sorry I didn't notice earlier." He took her hand and swung it possessively as they walked.

The sea was grey and very calm, lapping and sucking at their feet as it ran over the glycerine sand. Far out, the squat silhouette of a container ship moved slowly as though pulled by wires against the dimming backdrop of the sky. Her heart began to thump and she thought, is this how it starts? Love?

When he said abruptly, "Let's go and sit up on the big dune," she nodded and they began to walk across the beach towards the familiar humped shape near the river mouth. They had made a hideout behind there years ago, down a tunnel of thorny bush in a small sandy clearing where the sun broke through and the pounding of the sea was muffled.

He climbed ahead of her, pulling at her hand.

"I wonder if the hideout's still there?" She looked up at him smiling, expecting to see him smile too at the memory. She wished she could prolong the climb by slowing their movements to the dreamlike pace of a slow-motion film.

"Probably overgrown." He did not slow down or smile, but forged upwards, tugging impatiently at her hand.

14

When they reached the top, she was clammy and breathless. Her hair clung to her cheeks. "Here," he said, "here, sit on my shirt," and wrenching open his buttons, pulled it off to spread it on the wind-rippled sand. She sat down and put her arms round her knees and looked away down the beach, a little embarrassed by the flamboyance of his gesture.

He thumped down beside her. She turned her head and was about to say something about the haze that hung over the sea, when he flung his arm round her shoulders and pulled her against his bare chest.

All the way along the beach since he took her hand, she had been imagining Kenny wanting to kiss her, but gently, in the wry affectionate way that former lovers and old friends always did in books when they met again years later. Not this hard crushing of lips, nor the feel like an electric shock of his tongue forcing her teeth apart.

She pulled away, gasping, but the arm tightened and he twisted his body to push her down on the shirt. She felt the sand gritting under her head. He said hoarsely, rolling his weight on top of her, "Come on, kiss me."

Sweat prickled on her upper lip. She tasted salt and the faint sweetness of his alien spit. "Oh please, don't." She managed to get the words out past the rasping stubble on his cheek. Her lips moved stiffly. "Please, Kenny."

He drew back. "What's wrong with you? Never been kissed? I'll show you how." Before she could answer his mouth came down again and his body seemed to spread over her, locking her in a tight cage of bone and muscle.

In fright, she freed her arms and clawed at his back with her nails, at the same time trying to thrust a knee up into his groin, remembering that it was supposed to hurt a man. He gave a sudden grunt and pushed her away. "Jeez, what's that for?"

"I didn't ask you to attack me!" She sat up, brushing away the sand grains caked round her mouth.

"You weren't exactly reluctant."

Bewildered, she said, "I never knew kissing could be like that."

"You're wasting my time, then." He turned a sullen back on her. There were red marks where she had scratched him. "Go on, run away home back to Mummy."

She crawled to her feet and stumbled down the sandy slope over the fleshy tendrils of the dune creepers. Hot tears blurred her eyes.

She did not see, until she reached the relative flatness of the beach, the dark motionless figure of the fisherman waiting for her.

He held out his hand. "I found your watch on the rocks."

"What?" In her distress she did not remember the watch she had lost.

"Your watch. I tried to give it back before, but you ran away. Here."

Over the susurrus of the waves she heard a thudding of feet in the sand and Kenny walked past, tucking his shirt untidily into his shorts.

Helen did not look at him. Through a lens of tears she could see only the never-to-be-forgotten expression on the fisherman's face.

Jenny Hobbs was born in Durban, attended Natal schools, and holds a B.A. from the University of Natal, Pietermaritzburg. Her short stories have been published in *Contrast*, and in South African and overseas anthologies, and have been broadcast by the SABC and BBC. She has worked as a freelance journalist for the past twenty years, including four on the women's section of *Bona* magazine. She wrote a humorous column for *Darling* magazine, a selection from these writings appeared in her first book, *Darling Blossom*. Her novel, *Thoughts in a Makeshift Mortuary*, was a finalist for the 1989 CNA Literary Award. *The Sweet-smelling Jasmine* was selected for Publisher's Choice in 1993. Both novels are to appear in German translation. She lives in Johannesburg.

Patrick Waldo Davids

Wings for Bulbie

"The name is Smith, George Smith, teacher by profession and South African Breweries supporter by choice," our new Maths teacher introduced himself. He was small but had a booming voice. Across the road the old church clock echoed the hour as if to emphasise that it was the beginning of a new school year *and* the first Maths period.

Sheer silence. As if a question had been asked and no one knew the answer. For the very first time I realised that the blue-gum trees, planted by the town fathers, exuded a terrible stench.

"This odd, pot-bellied toppie a teacher? Our new Maths teacher? No ways, old pally, seems more like a first class weekend alcoholic to me. Supply him with a plug and a live wire and he's a bulbie," J.J., a real troublemaker and the school's Mathematics whizz, whispered as Bulbie introduced the Maths syllabus.

"Anything on your mind, Mister . . .?" Bulbie asked, looking J.J. level in the eye.

"John Jansen, Sir, but plain J.J. for my *bras*. No, I was just saying: looks like a year of suffering," J.J. retorted. The class sniggered.

"Negative attitude, Mister J.J.," Bulbie said and turned to the rest of the class. "To quote Bogart: I think it's the start of a beautiful friendship, but then, it has to come from both sides." He conveyed the message with the appropriate hand movements.

Bulbie's introduction of himself soon reached the bush telegraph – as happens in most small towns. His inevitable fall from grace soon became the latest jigsaw puzzle for the small-town toppies and aunties. You see, a drunkard-teacher, and what's more, one that prided himself on it, simply *had* to succumb in a missionary town with prohibition bred in the bone. The only missing pieces in the puzzle were how, where and when.

Bulbie had scarcely been in town for a month, when the vultures started circling above his head. "Talks and dresses like a school master, but the look in the eye and the behaviour and everything else reek of a brandy-breath that hides behind peppermint bubblegum. Anyway, seems like his liver'll be finished long before his career," I overheard a neighbour and my mother gossiping over the fence one afternoon.

Bulbie started winning us over with his humour. "Chewing snot once again!" his voice would boom through the classroom whenever we screwed up. A voice more poisonous than the cane. Even the frequency with which J.J. tried his luck, seemed to be diminishing.

But there were those who were waiting for the vultures to land.

Our first big assignment followed. We were speechless: "Sorry, Sir, but this *is* the Maths class, isn't it?" Eddie the Philosopher tried to be smart when he heard what Bulbie wanted.

"Time will tell, Mister Eddie," Bulbie replied with a shrug.

You see, each of us had to write an essay on a person who had influenced modern Mathematics. And for us this had sweet blow-all to do with figures. That afternoon, I gathered the entire class in the library where we brainstormed about what Bulbie was expecting from us.

"This guy might scheme he's funny – with this essay-thing – but I'll show him that I'm not stupid." Eddie expressed almost everyone else's attitude.

The next week, Bulbie had our essays read out to the class for comment. "All mathematicians are dope-heads," J.J. vented his frustration with a frown, when we had finished listening.

"Something like that, Mister J.J., except these guys didn't need boosters, they were spontaneous dreamers who moved boundaries," Bulbie said and put us on a trip of our own. He had us look into the world of Einstein, Newton and many others. The achievements and the disappointments, which the newly-found knowledge often carried in its wake. How scientists were seen as the Antichrist in the Middle Ages, and how they were hunted because of their revolutionary ideas. How Jules Verne wrote about travelling to the moon (in a boat propelled by birds) decades before man set foot on its surface . . .

"If you can dream it, ladies and gentlemen, you can do it. Maths is more than an exact science. It's the quest for answers to questions which affect human existence."

The class stared at Bulbie as if he were hanging on a Christmas tree – and some of them wished he would fuse. I could read it on their faces.

Then one Friday afternoon, J.J. and co. put Bulbie in a humiliating situation. They had pinched some bottles of brandy from his car, opened them and poured the contents into a big plastic bag. They then, craftily and strategically, hung the bag from one of the many gum trees in the parking area – right above Bulbie's car. The bag was tied in such a way that it would release a brandy-shower on Bulbie the moment the door on the driver's side was opened.

Then they spread the news: Come and watch, Bulbie's going to be taught a lesson!

Needless to say, that afternoon, for a change, the students were in no hurry to get home when the bell rang. They didn't wait in vain – the contraption worked perfectly. Some of the guys laughed and others just stood there, shaking their heads.

The blow to my ego is worse than being soaked with brandy, said Bulbie's facial expression amid peals of laughter from the others in the shade of the blue-gums.

It was clear – there was more to this revenge than the essay-writing business. There must have been instigators. Somewhere the grown-ups had a hand in the brandy-bath story. Clearly, the message to Bulbie was: Master Bulbie, conform your behaviour and change your views on life, or suffer!

"Ladies and gentlemen, the world is more than a teachers' diploma, a university degree or a safe but unsatisfactory existence," was one of the mottos in Bulbie's motivation bible. And it was one motto too many and too dangerous.

"The Lord's mercy's like a shot of brandy, mighty powerful, so you want to say no thank you, yet the guarantee of salvation beckons and you swallow," a *babalaas* Bulbie would greet us most Mondays. Then he would rest his tired eyes upon each of us for a few moments, before opening his briefcase and taking out his Maths textbook.

But when he entered the classroom the Monday after that fateful Friday, he said: "My daddy was a travelling salesman when my brothers and I were tiny tots. He would always return home late in the afternoon, usually after three weeks on the road, and greet us boys with a helluva box of Smarties and Mamma with a kiss. The Smarties he would strew on the lawn (usually a jungle by the time he returned). We would then rush outside and, on all fours, start looking for our treasure with the eagerness of field mice. Of course the two wanted to be alone, wanted us out of the way to be able to enjoy the reunion. My daddy underestimated our intelligence. He could have told us directly.

Ladies and gentlemen, have I ever underestimated your intelligence? So please, don't throw Smarties on my lawn. If you want to tell me something or humiliate me, say or do it directly," Bulbie concluded.

Then he opened the Maths textbook and never said another word about the incident.

But the Smarties-on-the-lawn story was gnawing at our consciences. After all, we felt for Bulbie. Even J.J. – although he would never have admitted it. Most of us were on Bulbie's side.

"Sir, my dad says you might be well-read and well-travelled, but you are preaching ungodly principles." The dominee's daughter aired her opinion one morning after another of Bulbie's provocative statements. Bulbie was amused. Nothing more.

His arrival in our little town had started not only a battle with our own consciences, but also with the beliefs of our parents. After several differences and infights our class came to an agreement. A few weeks later, we collected enough money among ourselves for a couple of bottles of brandy. We wrapped and ribboned them and with an apology (J.J. was the first to sign) left them on Bulbie's table on the last day of term. He thanked the class with a Smartie-hunt-smile as token of reconciliation. And with "The world's your oyster. And oh yes, ladies and gentlemen, please practise safe sex during the vacation," he took leave of us.

"Hey guys, they're going to close shop on Bulbie if we don't do something," Eddie, the principal's *laaitie*, said to the class one Friday, some weeks later. "Apparently, Monday is D-day."

A Save Bulbie Campaign was immediately launched. And on Sunday afternoon, with the eternal gum tree stench in my nostrils, I went to Bulbie's house.

As I walked through the front gate, I noticed the empty brandy bottle on the stoep table. Bulbie was sitting on the *riempiesbank*, staring at the stone floor. Through the open sash window I caught a glimpse of his wife sitting dejectedly in an armchair. On a small table in the corner of the stoep was a photo of a *laaitie* my age. A photo with a black ribbon across one corner.

"Sir, I'm here on behalf of the class," I heard myself say.

"Aha, my Maths class whose so-called coloured teacher's under the influence on the Sabbath – definitely in a different category, like a donkey in the Durban July," he slurred sarcastically. "You see that *laaitie* in the picture? Of course you see. My son. There's a lot that the holier-than-thou prohibitionists and moral guardians do not know. Paul, my only son, the one who had to give wings to my dreams. They brought the news during the riots. He'd hung himself in his cell. Suicide. And then the windowdress investigation, the post-mortem, identification and funeral. My heart screamed foul play, but my mind rebelled. The wife was destroyed; never been the same. My bottle-therapy is the quick-charge type – it instantly washes away the guilt and sorrow.

"So, now you know that your master Bulbie, the spontaneous dreamer, and your unwilling hero, has feet of clay."

I could see tears in those well-read and well-travelled eyes, so I turned my face away. "Sir, we'll support you on Monday," I promised.

Then I fled from the stoep. The gum tree stench suddenly reminded me of the slaughtered ox whose stinking guts I saw bulging out when I was six.

That Monday in October was more than merely blue.

We milled around in front of the principal's office with a poster stating our demand: Mr Smith stays or the school is a riot zone.

Two hours later the clearly tense principal and school committee announced: Mr Smith could stay – on certain terms.

He had to go to a rehabilitation centre for two months and on his return, the committee would again consider his case.

I shuffled towards Bulbie who was observing the happenings from a distance. "Didn't I promise?" I tried to boost my own mood.

Bulbie looked at me. "Now your hero wishes for wings –," he said, but his voice was cold, as if he were far away already.

Despite undergoing treatment in the rehabilitation centre, Bulbie left town at the end of the year. About two months later his wife phoned to tell me about the accident. The police report apparently read: *Collided head-on with a tree while under the influence of alcohol.*

"The day George died was our Paul's birthday," Mrs Smith added, and then hung up.

"You know, Bulbie already died that Monday in October," Eddie said when I told him. "Executed by a firing squad of fans and followers. By us."   *L. K.*

Patrick Waldo Davids was born on a missionary station in the southern Cape in 1970. When he was three, the family moved from Tergniet to Groot Brakrivier, where he completed his schooling. Between 1989 and 1992 he was a B.A. student at Stellenbosch, hesitating between Law and Journalism. Until it was dissolved in late 1994, Patrick worked with the George Peace Committee. He has since returned to Stellenbosch to complete his LL.B. degree. Despite a cool reception given by school "bras" to his first short story in 1987, he has decided that writing (or scribbling) is for him. With this story he makes his début as fiction writer.

Sandile Memela

A life besieged

When it came to concealing his troubles, Sizwe Sakhile was no less capable than the next educated black man. At least he thought so, and there was a certain amount of evidence to back him up. He always had a happy expression on his face – no, not quite – more of a subtle smile. Also, he was the sophisticated, urbanised type, wearing a tie, a white shirt and neat pants and that gave him an advantage. It was harder to know how he felt and what made his heart tick.

He came through the gate to the big school yard to park his car, and he believed, and hoped, that he looked passably well. It was a matter of sheer hope because there was not much that he could add to his present effort. As he locked the door he glanced up, expecting to see the principal taking his case from the passenger seat of his own car. They often met at this hour, just a few minutes before the first students started trickling in. If Sizwe worried about his appearance, it was mainly to impress the principal. Today there was no car and no principal. And also no students. Sizwe turned his head and the long grey stoep opened up before him. Wearily he trod over the paving stones that could have done with a scrub and shine.

To the left, the grass was a little wet. Flowers half stood and the trees looked half-alive, and in his immediate surroundings Sizwe sensed a lack of life and the sneaky presence of death. For a moment he thought he heard the screams of students running helter-skelter with the police hard at their heels, beating, whipping, kicking, punching. But there was nothing and he continued down the stoep.

Most of the staff at the school were in their early forties, a handful were over fifty. Lately, unless the weather was too cold or wet or the air too full of tear gas, they sat tight inside the lounge – as they called the staff room – and waited. Among these people Sizwe felt out of place. He was comparatively young, in his early twenties, and fresh from the University of Fort Hare. He was tall and always dressed like a movie star. His back was heavy and strong, but he stooped a little from sitting too long behind his desk during his student days.

Every morning shortly after eight, the teachers arrived and moved up and down the staff room making tea. They sat down on the old sofas and leather armchairs and began to gossip and look into the papers. They had nothing to do but wait out the day. Things were not normal at school these days.

Sizwe was used to keeping his head when others lost theirs, and even when chaos erupted, he always managed to keep his students busy with constructive work. But for the past three months, because there were no students and he had no option, he kept up his morale simply by praying that things would return to normal. He woke up as before the boycotts and was on the premises on time. He borrowed a paper from a colleague and scanned through the police report and general unrest pictures. Then he waited, waited for word from the DET in Pretoria. Sometimes he would take out a cigarette, drink a cup of black coffee and afterwards go out onto the school grounds. There was no business to attend to. He realised that this was draining life out of him, and of late he had become anxious. He was aware that this routine was not about to break up soon and he sensed that there was a big, dark cloud hovering over his head. What did the future hold for him? For the pupils? The country?

Before the end of the month he would know.

Today, as on previous days, Sizwe followed his daily course and crossed the street to the shebeen nearby.

Thami, the man who owned the shebeen, had an eye for class, and Sizwe was well aware of it. Thami's rather dull eyes lit up whenever he appreciated a thing of beauty, be it a garment or a woman. He, too, dressed well. It did not seem necessary since he was at his home most of the time, running the business. Still, he dressed well. Sizwe noticed he had on rich brown flannels, with a leather belt tightening his thickened waist, and an open-necked shirt.

Thami seemed not to see Sizwe approaching. He was looking thoughtfully out of the window at the main road, which was visible several houses away. Ben Naudé Drive, the neighbourhood's great thoroughfare, was the busiest road in the township and stretched for kilometre after kilometre. It was the road that led to all parts of the township and was used by taxis, buses, cars, casspirs, pedestrians, vans and lorries. It was forever teeming with life. Everybody, young and old, including the police and security forces, knew the ups and downs of the busiest street in the location.

This morning, however, Ben Naudé Drive looked like a deserted small-town street. It was quiet and tense, with an old man standing at the opposite gate to the shebeen, peering out like Thami to assess the situation.

"Do you think things will ever be like in the good old days?" Thami asked when Sizwe entered the shebeen.

"Oh, I don't know. Looks like we've passed the point of no return."

Only then Thami turned to look at Sizwe. "That's a real knock-out shirt you got on," he said and his eyes gleamed approval. "Where's it from?"

"A boutique, in the Rosebank Mall."

Even when he was troubled, Sizwe could still twist his lips in a pleasing way. The slow, sensuous movement of his youthful face was very attractive and he knew it. He went back a step, as if to stand away from himself and get a better look at his glamorous image in the long mirror on the wall full of advertisements, pictures of the latest brands of wine and spirits and beer, and faces of famous names in the modelling world. His glance was comic, yet tinged with tension; a comment on his situation. During his last years at university, when he wore the same pair of jeans day in and day out and his acquaintances would whisper that they were the only pants he had, he would carry on as if it did not bother him. Sizwe could still pretend that he was not tormented or suffering.

"I like this type of material," he said in his sociable, good-natured way. "It is wash and wear. You can send it to the cleaners if you want, but then it never smells as good as when it's washed. Plus if you wash it you save money. What with the economy as it is . . ."

Sizwe had not bought the shirt himself. It was a present from his girlfriend – his ex-girl – with whom he had fallen out because she was not college-educated. But there was no reason why he should tell Thami everything. Although perhaps Thami knew. He was the type of man who knew, and knew, and knew. People came to his place to talk about their problems, to drink and to forget. Sizwe also knew many things about Thami, for that matter, about Thami's wife and Thami's business, Thami's shady dealings and his health. None of these could be mentioned, so there was a great weight of the unspoken which left them little to talk about.

"Well, you smell good and are looking pretty grand today. I am sure all the women will be giving you a wink," Thami said.

And Sizwe said eagerly, "Do I? Do you really think so?" He glanced again at his reflection in the long mirror but he thought he didn't look good enough. A wide wrinkle appeared on his forehead. He involuntarily began fingering his light perm, half amused at his image on the wall. Then, suddenly, he felt a thrust of pride at what he had achieved so far. *You fighter, you survivor!* That was how he saw himself. He felt the sting of tear gas in his eyes, the whipping and beatings, the expulsion, the food boycotts and days of starving. There was the jailing of student leaders, and the blood amidst all the peaceful protest.

It was not easy to get where I am, he reflected. I could have done hard labour all my life. Or I could have ended up in the factories and become an extension of a machine. Instead, I fought against all types of odds to be what I wanted to be. And yet . . .

He had given his all, put in plenty of effort, content to sleep fewer hours. In high school, because of his understanding of the situation in the land, he had realised that he was doomed to poverty all his life – unless he resorted to one of the few remaining outlets of escape: Bantu Education. So, for six years, stubbornly, he had burnt the midnight candle at Madibane High in Diepkloof. He had spent Sunday afternoons at school while others visited shebeens and went to the stadium, music festivals and parties. He continued studying at the height of the exam boycotts. When the boycotts were called off at last, it was very late and difficult for those who had already started working in factories to return to school. As he knew it would be.

"I didn't see you here on Saturday," said Thami.

"Oh, I spent the night in town."

"Was it good?"

"I enjoyed it, although I must admit that this time I spent more than my pocket could afford."

During the past few years more and more young township professionals had been spending weekends at city hotels, bars, restaurants, because of the winds of change blowing over the country, and Sizwe had become one of them. Although he could not afford this way of life, he had to pursue it to keep up his image among his peers. He could not afford to lose a cent of his money any more, yet he was under eternal siege. He could not win or escape. Not once. And while the losses were great there weren't any gains. He was tired of losing, but tired also of the deplorable, oppressive living conditions, and so he had to lead a double life.

"Oh," said Thami, "I had a short visit from some 'comrades' over the weekend. They really scared the hell out of me."

"What did they want this time?"

"They ordered me to stop operations for a while. You know the stuff about mourning the dead and boycotting white-owned businesses."

Sizwe nodded. "What are you going to do?"

"Oh hell, I don't know. Who knows what to do nowadays? We're literally being dictated to by the security forces on the one hand and school kids on the other. All I know is that I have to pay rent, feed my family and make a living." It seemed necessary for Thami to thrust his hands deep into his pockets. Sizwe saw his hands turn into fists.

"That doesn't sound so good. You come across as a man who is prepared to live under a permanent state of emergency." Sizwe had meant to be conversationally playful, but his voice was toneless and his eyes, slack and buried under his brows, wandered off. He did not want to hear more. He did not want to hear from anybody else about the unbearable burden of being black. Maybe Thami already knew what to do next, he consoled himself, being the sort of man who knew, and knew, and knew.

No, it wasn't good. Life was unfair. What turned out to be right for one was wrong for another. Sizwe held out a bank note and asked Thami for a beer. He and Thami poured the amber liquid from the two sweating cold bottles that already stood on the table at 9:30 a.m. and began drinking.

In the tense morning atmosphere outside the sun continued to shine. Life went on.

Born in Alexandra Township, Johannesburg, in 1962, Sandile Memela went to Ekuthuleni Primary, then Immaculata High in Diepkloof. Matriculating in 1980, he enrolled for a B.A. (Communication) at Fort Hare, but was expelled in 1982 for participating in a boycott. In 1986, he obtained a B.A. in Journalism from Stellenbosch University. He joined *City Press* as senior political journalist, and was appointed arts editor in 1991. In 1989 he was short story finalist in the Bertrams VO Literary Award for African Literature and an African Writers' Association award. He has contributed to *Tribute, True Love, Thandi, Jive, The Sowetan, The Star* and *Sunday Times*. He lives in Soweto.

27

Hein Willemse

A dark girl in Tepotzlán

"Congratulations on your appointment, exile!" Nikki shouted at the end of the passage. "The top brass like you. Now at least you've got permanency!"

"Thanks."

"You deserve it!" She sealed her wishes with a smacking kiss. "How did the director just put it? 'You are now a *full* member of the *famous* Centre for Asian and African Studies, and may I add, at the *prestigious* Colégio de México!'" She smiled. "What a whimp! Hang on, before I forget: have you read your favourite journalist this morning?"

"Who?"

"Escobar in *El Tiempo*."

"No, I don't read that excuse for a journalist any longer."

"He's onto your Mandela this time." She took a newspaper clipping from her sling bag.

> I would also like to see Mandela free, but his freedom will last only as long as his propaganda value. Prison is his best political stage and also his best insurance policy. I am entirely for the liberation of blacks, just as I am for the rights and self-respect of Indians. However, before majorities are granted equal rights, they must first know how to use those new rights. Freedom above all. Yes, but also freedom from barbarism and illiteracy. Anything less is the exchange of one form of oppression for another.

She pushed the piece of newspaper into my hand. "You just can't escape from his kind. So brazen!"

"Bloody racist!"

"It's no use. Escobar's got you again. You must be the only one he still manages to upset. We've all given up hope long ago."

"It freaks me out. At least under apartheid they covered up this kind of rubbish, but here he's writing without anyone opposing him."

"That's freedom of speech," Nikki said resignedly. "Why are you so put out by him? What are you going to do this time? Write another letter? So that the man can again correct every bit of your Spanish: first learn my language before you take me on, sir!"

"What am I doing here if I can't even oppose Escobar? I planted bombs against apartheid. I was hounded and thrown into jail. Now I'm teaching quietly in your freedom, as if everything is okay. In the meantime, you allow Escobar under the guise of freedom of speech to slander all and everybody!"

"Cool it. It's not worth it. What are you doing on Saturday?"

"Where is your Latino passion!?"

"Forget about Escobar. Cool it. I'm not wasting my energy on a rat. What are you doing on Saturday?"

"Nothing. I've only got to mark a couple of political theory essays."

"Well, then you're coming along. We'll celebrate your new job on El Tepozteco." She slung her bag over her shoulder and turned slightly as she left to shout back, "And stop fretting!"

"I'm hungry," Nikki said soon after we arrived in the village of Te-potzlán. "I know the best eating place here." We strolled along the cobbled lanes to the street market on the *zocálo* in front of the old Dominican cathedral. "*This* is my Mexico. The market and its people. There's a woman whom I visit regularly. She speaks the most beautiful Nahuatl." A slightly built woman with a bright neck scarf waved in our direction. "There she is!" They recognised each other through the sea of multicoloured awnings. The woman eagerly pulled some camp stools from under a table with a red plastic cloth. She smiled and looked at me with surprise.

"You're a stranger. Are you a Cuban? Well, then you must try our own *huitlacoche*. It's pre-Columbian," she said, "and truly Indian."

"Very well," I agreed.

Unlike the dark Nikki, a spitting image of the actress Sonia Braga, she reminded me of my past in the Bo-Kaap: something of the warm-heartedness, something of the colourful Muslim women at their sa-mosa stalls along Wale Street on Saturdays.

"*Huitlacoche*." The woman spooned a greyish black slimy mixture onto a tortilla. "Enjoy it! It's great."

29

Nikki smiled. "It's true, it's really great. Not tinned stuff. This is the people's chow."

"We make it from the black mushroom that grows on maize. It doesn't cost anything to pick, and even less to prepare," our hostess offered in the way of information. Then she switched over and continued talking to Nikki in the sweet-sounding ancient language of this inland region. It was a cordial conversation that I could not even begin to understand.

I ate reluctantly, trying hard not to show my distaste. If they saw my discomfort, they paid no attention to it. Nikki ordered another one and yet another. There was no dog nearby to quietly relieve me of my helping. Only good manners forced me to swallow the formless mixture on the pink plastic plate and pay my debt to the Indian gods. Nikki was enjoying her visit. She ordered more, this time *flor da clabaza*, vegetables and tortilla. Even though this dish looked better, I couldn't rid myself of my conditioning. I was embarrassed at my prejudices.

"It's so good, but you've hardly eaten anything."

"I'm not hungry," was the only way to cut short Nikki's insistence.

> But which blacks are to be set free? Those who have remained behind in the Stone Age or those who live with white people, like the Jews in Russia or the West Indians in South London? If blacks in Africa want to multiply without restraint, grant them the freedom then to wipe themselves out. Experience teaches us that they will do this with great gusto.

El Tepozteco, the inhabitants' sacred mountain, towered above the dilapidated church building. The eroded masonry looked like septic wounds. "It's seventeenth century. Look at the façade," Nikki said next to me.

"Yes, it's impressive."

"It won't disintegrate easily. Look, the pillars are more than a metre thick."

"Think of all the sweat that must have gone into it."

"I can't think of the Church without thinking of our people's suffering. It sounds somewhat melodramatic, but it's true." We peeped into the building. A wedding was in progress. Nikki spoke without looking in my direction. "It was actually the Church that colonised us."

"This is something we also know."

"Yes. How does your Bishop Tutu put it? We had the land and the settlers the Bible."

"Now we've got the Bible and the settlers the land."

Nikki gave a hearty laugh of recognition. At the entrance she drew the visitors' book towards her. "You must be the only South African who has ever visited this place. Today, in solidarity, I am also from South Africa." With a flourish she wrote our names in the visitors' book and next to them *Sudáfrica*. "Are you proud to be a South African?"

A young girl came running in our direction. "Oh, please come and help!"

Nikki's question was lost. "What's wrong?" she asked. "Has something happened?"

"No, please come and help. You're tall. Please come and help us tie the bell." The girl pushed a brightly-decorated cardboard bell into my arms. In front of the massive church door a sturdy chap was waiting. He squatted and helped me onto his shoulders. I hung the bell in the middle of the two-and-a-half metre door-frame. The brass band was warming up. They played a few chords and paced up and down impatiently. A group of *mariachis* with tight-fitting embroidered black trousers played their string instruments and sang a ballad in honour of the bridal couple.

We walked back to the monastery. "You can feel honoured," said Nikki. "You have hung the bell on the door."

"What's in the bell?"

"Confetti and rice. It's our own little ritual, adapted over the years."

The entrances to the building were small and the walls were solid. The centuries-old red tiled floor was worn. Despite the decay, the neatness struck me. We ascended the bell tower until we looked down onto the front of the church. Together with the band we waited for the bridal couple to appear.

"Do you think that people ever had sex here?"

Nikki smiled. "Of course. The Spaniards might have colonised us with their Church, but our human nature they could certainly not destroy. As you know, some of our priests had quite a number of children. Yet today they are national heroes."

31

"*Aqui estacionado Maria*," I read the graffiti on the walls.

Nikki laughed at the irreverence. "Yes, in spite of Mother Mary's pious sanctity. The Church gave us discipline and marriage." The bridal couple emerged smiling and stood around self-consciously in front of the massive door. The bridegroom shuffled about uneasily. Then he touched the bride with a complacent pink smile. A family member in exotic blue was arranging the pageboy for the official photograph. The *mariachis* sang heartily. The bridegroom pulled the cord of the bell and confetti spilled over them. The spectators applauded. Two little girls giggled while they picked up rice and confetti and threw it at the bridal couple. "It's her second marriage," Nikki suddenly said.

"How do you know?"

"Social codes, a Mexican just knows them. It's her dress and the kind of wedding."

The bride smiled and lightly tugged at her companion. They climbed onto a decorated mule cart and commenced their honeymoon with the blare of the brass band and a sudden burst of fire crackers. "They'll first go into town to announce their wedding. Then they'll go up to El Tepozteco to give thanks and ask for a blessing. Look at the dark clouds. They'll have to be quick."

We descended. I wondered about the lives of the ancient predecessors of the Church. There was no written information that the visitor could consult. In the cool courtyard we passed a well and a bed of roses. "I experience it everywhere," I complained, "that the Mexicans don't really take the tourist into consideration."

There was an uneasy pause, then Nikki said in a low voice: "In the end everything is for ourselves. If the tourist benefits from it, fine. But firstly it is for ourselves. It's because we want to be independent. Do you see the well and the battlements above? Ironically, even today we have to protect ourselves against the imperialists, just as the monks once had to protect themselves against the Indians."

I realised that I had touched Nikki's nationalistic threshold. Together with the last row of wedding guests we left the church grounds. "If after five years here you still feel like a tourist, then you must now start buying souvenirs," she said.

"I'm sorry. I didn't mean it in that way."

"Then I'll be the tourist." I heard the bite in her voice. "I'm looking for salad servers." The vendors were packing up before the

32

threatening storm. She gave me a sideways glance and a muscle pulled in her cheek. "For the bourgeoisie it's kitsch – all these salad bowls, but we like them. We like our kitsch."

The first thunder rumbled over the dome of the cathedral. The couple on their bridal wagon raced over the deserted *zocálo* and the fire cracker salute of their guests could not be distinguished from the thunder.

> The whites of South Africa have laboured to construct one of the most developed economies in the world. It is their every right to be proud and unyielding. In a distant corner of the world's chess board a white castle keeps at bay a thundering line of black pawns. But whatever move it makes, the players have already planned its fall in favour of other more valuable pieces. What a fitting game for the end of the century!

"We won't be able to climb El Tepozteco now," Nikki interrupted my thoughts. "It'll be raining soon. We can't be caught on the mountain. Perhaps another time." She put the salad servers in her sling bag and said goodbye to the vendor in Nahuatl.

On the way home, just outside Tepoztlán, the Beetle's wipers gave in with the first downpour. "This as well," Nikki sighed. "I'd rather not risk it. Let's turn back before we're washed away, car and all." We drove back to a little bar on the square. Later, through the heavy showers and thunder, we heard string music.

"It comes from the church," I said. "Let's go and see." We sprinted through the rain towards the sound of the music. Two girls were practising the mandolin and the harp. The music was enchanting. "One can only be silent."

The dome amplified the sound to an indescribable intensity. We listened in silence, Nikki with her feet on the pew in front of her. A shiver went down my spine: it was as if the pure chords pierced through a haze. When the girls stopped, Nikki turned to me.

"You cannot walk away from such music." She nudged me. "That's what we came back for, not because of the rain."

"Don't tell me you now believe in fate?"

"Perhaps. For this music and this atmosphere I can almost become a Christian again. This is the closest the Church will ever come to comforting me. This music, this atmosphere . . ."

Nikki pulled her legs up to her chin. "I stopped being a Catholic a long time ago, but I still like the rituals. We have made the staunch old Catholic church our own, with our own symbols. Take the story of this picture, for example." She pointed to an icon, a dark-toned Mary-like image, between the half-burnt candles above the altar.

"The Virgin of Guadalope?"

"Yes, do you know the story?" she asked without really expecting an answer.

"No, not quite."

"That was the time when the Spaniards tried to convert us but with little success. Until one day when a boy picked a bunch of rare roses in an inaccessible place and carried it in his cloak to his bishop. On the way he was overcome by an inexplicable drowsiness and dreamed about a holy virgin talking to him. In his own language, in Nahuatl. When he got to his bishop, there was an image of the same radiant virgin inside his cloak. For the Church this was a miracle. *La Morenita*, the dark girl who was to become the Virgin of Guadalope. Millions were converted then. Now the entire Latin America crawls before our own Morenita." She paused. "The storm has passed. We must go."

We walked out into the smell of damp soil and rain. The sky had cleared and the stifling afternoon heat had evaporated. It was like the cleansing of a Karoo storm. A stream of brown water rushed down the cobbled road in front of the *zocálo*.

A white castle keeps at bay a thundering line of pawns.

"We must go. It'll be dark soon," Nikki said while I wiped the windscreen with my handkerchief.

We drove up the mountain pass and looked down on to the Tepoztlán Valley.

"It's a pity about El Tepozteco. We'll have to come again."

"Wait, pull over," I said just before we crossed over the top back to Mexico City.

"No, I'll not be able to come back soon. I'm going back to South Africa."

She opened her mouth, but no sound came out.

"I'm glad you brought me here to this place."

34

I looked back. The mist around the mountain top had cleared, but the little town with its red-tiled roofs remained shrouded in dense green forest.   *P. B.*

Born in Ladismith, Cape Province, Hein Willemse completed his high school career in Worcester. He studied at the University of the Western Cape. He has published poetry and short stories in South African and overseas magazines. The collection of poetry called *Angsland* appeared in 1982. He is a founder member of the Congress of South African Writers, and is on the editorial staff of various literary and academic publications. He is currently associate professor in South African literature in the Department of Afrikaans at UWC and lives in Somerset West.

Lindsay King

A garbage story

We left the house at 28 Carnation Avenue in Bishop Lavis, roaring with laughter. It was a sizzling hot Friday in the summer of 1993.

Everything started with a complaint from a Bishop Lavis resident about garbage that had not been removed for nearly two weeks. My editor assigned me to the job early that morning, but since it was a busy day with one deadline after another, it was only at about 4:30 that afternoon that Leon, one of our photographers, and I made our way across town to cover the story. It was only my third job on the streets and the thought of a front page byline spurred me on. Being the greenest reporter at a local newspaper in the Mother City, I mostly got sent to cover less illustrious happenings, but that didn't bother me because I enjoyed shaking hands with the locals.

Thinking back, I realise that a single mistake, that of forgetting the exact address back at the office, resulted in a story far more interesting than the one that was meant to be. Anyway, between Leon and myself, we figured it would not be that difficult to locate the garbage in Carnation Avenue.

At least, that's what we thought.

Several times we drove from one end of the avenue to the other, but could not detect a single trace of piled-up garbage on the sidewalk. Yet all the trash in the streets made me wonder whether a gale had not let Nature go its way and spread the pile all over the place! There were dirty pieces of material and old clothes, paper, plastic, old tins, garden refuse and more papers and plastic for as far as the eye could see. But this mess was not the unremoved waste we were looking for.

Anyway, it was a mean, hot Friday afternoon. We just wanted to get the job done and get back to the office as soon as possible. Though we stopped several times to ask residents whether they knew about the garbage, we had no luck. Both Leon and I got fed up with our mission and I decided to ask just one more person before relinquishing the search. I stopped the car next to a young woman with a baby.

36

Leon got out while I remained seated. From within the car I could not follow their conversation, but from the woman's facial expressions I soon gathered that she had no clue either.

Then, just as we were about to give up, a plump middle-aged woman with a stocking drawn over her hair, started waving madly at us from a window on the other side of a semi-detached house. She was obviously calling us over. Leon hurried across to her and I followed hopefully, but before we could even introduce ourselves, she started shooting words at us, faster than the speed of sound.

"Ek sê, is dis now de time to come? Jislaaik, man, I'm waiting here de whole day for you. You mos think I got nuffing else to do, hey? What de hell did you make so long for? Nay man, it's blerry pafetic dat one can't depent on anyone anymore. Look how late it is. It's five o'clock an I phone nine o'clock dis mawning! Don't just stand dere, come in!" she said and then promptly disappeared from the window.

Leon and I glanced at each other. We knew that this was going to be a tough one, but the fact that we seemed to be making progress was comforting. This woman was without doubt going to be a valuable source of information – for my first front page byline, I hoped.

We hurried back to the car where Leon grabbed his camera and I my notebook and pen. As we entered the living-room of the small house, some seven or more youngsters disappeared from the room. A damp, stale smell and three middle-aged women with a look of complaint on their heavily (and badly) painted faces were left behind. Leon remained standing in the doorway. We greeted the women and I sat down on one of the uncomfortable chairs. Just as I was about to befriend the women, the one with the stocking entered the room with a huge cardboard box, the weight of which was clearly taxing her arms.

"Dis de blerry limit! Afterall, I phoned you nine o'clock, I mean to say! Watse service is dit? I somma call your larnies about dis," she threatened as she tried not to drop the box.

"I'm terribly sorry but we had great difficulty finding your house since we . . ." I tried to explain.

"Nè? From nine dis mawning?" she snapped back sarcastically. "You dere, take de box! I'll tawk to him while you put it in de motor-car," she said to Leon and dumped the box in his hands.

Oh no! I thought. Does she expect us to take the garbage sample back with us and dump it somewhere? Is she loony?

"I'm sorry, but we only need to take a picture of you with the garbage, outside on the sidewalk," I said, trying to be polite.

"*Garbage*? You're right, dis *is* garbage, ou pal! I couldn't put it better myself. But ek sê, how quick can you fix dis blerry thing? De damn thing's been a hessle from de day I bought it. If I don't get it back on Monday, I want my money back or I'll sue you. If you came dis mawning, de blessit thing'd've been fixed olready. Jinne man, now I'll be whifout a TV for de whole weekend an my fayvrit sow is on tonight!"

The truth dawned slowly on Leon and me. We burst out laughing, leaving the woman and her friends even more confused.

The woman did not find our laughter amusing at all. "Now you're really making me de moer in! I sommer put dis in de papers or put daai kwaai Isabel Jones on you!" she said furiously at the top of her voice. And the other ladies agreed by nodding their heads. With shaking hands, our spokeswoman borrowed an "enchie" from her companions and lit it.

"Tell dem about de los knoppe. What's knoppe again?" one of the women asked.

"Buttons. Yes an de stripes on de screen is terribly *ge*-mix," the other one said and pointed at the box which Leon was still holding.

"You tell them," he gasped between bouts of laughter.

"Ladies . . . ladies, I have to explain . . ." I tried, but all in vain.

"I tell you de blerry thing's uselezz! I never bought such a piece of . . . uh . . ." She struggled to find the right word. "*Wat's gemors in Engels?*"

"Rubbies an garbitch," her friend helped her out.

At this stage I simply *had* to clear up the misunderstanding: "Ladies," I tried again, "we are from the *Cape Flats Herald* and this is a big misunderstanding. We were actually looking for someone who phoned us about garbage not being removed. When you called us in from the street we assumed it was you who had phoned."

But she still didn't register – since she was not really interested in what I had to say. Leon by now was convulsed with laughter and had to put down the box on the floor.

That put the cherry on the top for the poor woman. Or rather, the last straw on the camel's back. "Dammit, dat's enough! Jus take de blessit thing. I want my TV fixt. You're jus scared, you two, now you somma say you're from the papers." Then her mouth fell open and her eyes widened. "Hey man," she said, "... what do you mean you're from de *Herald*? From . . . from de *what*?"

"From the press," I tried to reply with as much dignity as I could muster.

"Ag nee . . .!" was all the embarrassed woman could utter as she finally realised her mistake. She covered her face with both hands, then she quickly pulled the stocking from her head and coyly tried to fix her wild, ungroomed hair (for the guys from the newspaper, you see).

"Haai, Mister, I'm sorry. But it's dat blerry broken TV. Haai, please don't put dis in de papers, hey man, promise me!"

The youngsters who had previously left the room and had since been quiet, were obviously tuned in to the happenings, because from the back of the house came peals of laughter. Even the three women had difficulty controlling their laughter, not minding that the tears running down their cheeks were ruining their make-up.

Whether the TV was ever fixed I will never know, but I must admit, I would never have thought that a broken TV, an unknown address and an unsatisfied customer could leave me with a "garbage story" and a displeased editor. I guess, when young are fresh in the business, you are apt to suffer from too great expectations!

As a matter of fact, it was a full three months after this little episode that I had my first front page byline, and a smiling editor.

Lindsay King was born in Stellenbosch in 1967, and matriculated at the Lückhoff Senior Secondary School. A passion for foreign languages was born during a visit to Germany and Austria in 1983; in 1989 he obtained a B.A. in German, Psychology and Dutch at the University of the Western Cape, and an Honours degree in German literature the next year. Then the travel bug bit again, and his travels included Canada, the United States and Britain. In 1992 he joined *Die Burger* as journalist. This is his first publication apart from newspaper writing. His great loves, in addition to German literature, are poetry and taking artistic photographs.

Johnny Masilela

Baba Mfundisi the clergyman

Half-asleep, a young boy staggered from one of the newly erected shacks at Boekenhoutfontein, carrying a baby in one arm.

Boekenhoutfontein has nothing to do with books, wood or a fountain, as the Afrikaans name may suggest. It is a piece of land on which the homeless have settled in their thousands since that new day dawned for South Africa.

The boy cringed at the blow of yet another hammer at work on yet another tin house rising in the neighbourhood, then planted his lips on the forehead of the baby, a bundle of joy wrapped in the most beautiful rags her parents could afford. The boy pulled the ill-fitting but craftily knitted pink woollen cap from the baby's eyes, at the same time putting back in place her nappy, a piece of cloth cut from an old school shirt.

The boy, with a complexion as black as the depths of a coal mine, was stark naked. Seemingly without a care in the world, he used his free hand to shield his eyes from the early morning sun. He staggered a few more steps into the sunshine, moved his free hand down to his little AK-47, and sent the urine in an arc through the empty air.

It was when the yellow liquid hit the leaves of a potted plant nearby, that Baba Mfundisi the clergyman drove by in his bakkie. The boy's misty eyes focused on the bearded man in his clerical collar, wearing a cassock decorated with images of the moon and the stars, and a multi-coloured head band made of strings of wool.

Baba Mfundisi waved at the boy and the baby and drove on.

Further down the street a Mozambican refugee with long fluffy hair leaned against a shack built of timber. The bright colour of his clothes was reminiscent of the carnival atmosphere of the streets of Maputo before the war. On the ground next to him stood a bottle of cheap brandy and a portable tape recorder switched on full blast. From time to time the Mozambican leapt into the air, gyrating to the fast rhythm of the Shangaan ballads.

Seeing Baba Mfundisi's bakkie cruising down the street, he

grabbed his bottle and the tape recorder and disappeared into the shack. Like many of the squatters, the Mozambican was a member of the Twelfth Apostle Christian Church of Jerusalem, headed by Baba Mfundisi.

The minister drove past, pretending not to see the new member from Mozambique dashing for the shelter of his shack. The bakkie rolled down the dusty street and turned into a corner where a group of youngsters were rolling dice. One of the boys gave a signal, warning fellow gamblers that Baba Mfundisi was approaching them.

The boys quickly scooped up the set of dice and the money, pretending nothing untoward was taking place. The minister brought his bakkie to a halt next to the youngsters. "What are you boys doing at a street corner on a day like this?" demanded Baba Mfundisi.

The boy closest to the bakkie replied they were discussing schoolwork.

"Good," muttered the minister, and continued towards a man and a woman at work on a maize patch. When the bakkie came to a halt in front of them and the minister got out, the two quickly dropped their implements and met the man of the cloth with embarrassed smiles. Baba Mfundisi was known to be against any form of manual work on a sacred day like Sunday. He gave them a steady look.

"We were just making touch-ups, you know," said the man of the house, touching the front of his old felt hat with one finger.

The minister ignored the man's excuses and asked if they were coming to the church, to which the man and his wife nodded enthusiastically.

"Baba Mfundisi, can I bring tea before you go?" asked the woman of the house, biting her fingernails.

"Tea, yes. That is very kind of you," replied Baba Mfundisi, and walked towards an empty sorghum beer crate in the shade of a morula tree.

"No, no, you cannot sit on that crate. I shall bring Baba Mfundisi a decent chair," protested the man, and disappeared into the shack. He returned with an old creaking chair which, he thought, was better under the circumstances than a beer crate.

A while later his wife emerged from the shack carrying a tray with the tea and boiled eggs. The minister had his tea and bid the man and woman of the house farewell, reminding them to join him at the church service. He then drove to the church, which was a bigger shack with a cross perched askance at the top, put up by his congregation as a temporary place of worship.

The shack stood on a piece of land on which the Twelfth Apostle Christian Church of Jerusalem congregation hoped to build a proper church, perhaps of red brick with a polished wooden cross and who knows, perhaps a huge church bell. Just like they have in the leafy suburbs of nearby Pretoria. Baba Mfundisi parked his bakkie in the shade of an acacia tree in the churchyard, and headed for the small church. Inside, members of the congregation were already humming hymns to the beat of a cowhide drum and the rhythmic tinkle of a little silver bell.

Shuffling his feet and moving his body to the rhythm of the drum and tinkling bell, Baba Mfundisi entered the church. Dancing his way through the rows of benches he finally reached the lectern. Baba Mfundisi raised his hand, ordering his flock to stop singing.

He paged through the Good Book, identified a favourite verse, and delivered an explosive sermon. His voice quivering, Baba Mfundisi broke into a trance, openly weeping for Jesus of Nazareth. "When the chief priests and officers saw him, they cried out, saying, Crucify him, crucify him . . . Hallelujah!"

"Hallelujah, praise the Lord!" responded the congregation, and a slight tinkling of the silver bell could be heard.

"Now there was set a vessel full of vinegar, and they filled a sponge with vinegar . . . and put it upon hysop, and put it to his mouth . . . Hallelujah!"

"Hallelujah, praise the Lord!"

"Then came the the soldiers, and brake the legs of the first, and of the other which was crucified with him . . . but when they came to Jesus, and saw that he was dead already, they brake not his legs . . . Hallelujah, amen . . ." At this point the church minister choked and trembled, hypnotised into a divine state of mind.

On realising the weeping priest could not continue, the cowhide drummer pounded his instrument, leading the charged congregation into another hymn.

Halfway through the singing and clapping of hands and the tinkling of the little bell, everything suddenly came to an eerie halt. When Baba Mfundisi came to, his tear-filled eyes looked down the muzzle of an AK-47 assault rifle. It was held very steadily by one of three young strangers that had entered the small church.

Dazed, Baba Mfundisi stared at the youth. At last he gathered enough courage and asked with a trembling voice: "What in the name of the Good Lord do you want, son?"

"The keys to the bakkie," replied the gunman, calmly.

Born in 1957 in the Holy Cross Mission Hospital outside Pretoria, Johnny Masilela grew up in the tobacco-farming district of Brits in the Western Transvaal, where his father headed a small school. He is presently a journalist, literary critic and columnist with *The Pretoria News*. His column is aimed, he says, at identifying aspects of black life beyond the political rhetoric. Johnny was inspired to try his hand at creative writing by those who have been following his column, among them Wendy Morgenrood, editor-in-chief of *Reader's Digest (SA)*. This is his first piece of fiction published in book form.

Dianne Case

The crossing

"You must buy lots of candles, Katy," her madam was saying. "We are going to see bloodshed that Africa has not seen yet. There will be no electricity, for how long, I'm not sure."

Strange how history repeats itself, she thought. She remembered how, when she herself was a girl of maybe eight years old, her own mother came home from work and told them, her little brother and herself, of the war that was "waiting over the water". Her mother's madam had told her then, as her madam was telling her now. She remembered that she and her little brother were so frightened, staring at the sky during the day, watching planes flying peacefully across the clear blue yonder and panicking that they were going to be bombed away, blown into tiny bits of blood spatterings.

How their father had laughed at their mother when he found the extra supplies she had sacrificed, hidden under their bed. And then their mother's earnest, almost tearful voice explaining, "There are Russian ships surrounding the coast. Mrs Fowler said so. We may be at war without knowing it."

Her father laughed even more at her mother's explanation. In no time he had sold the things she had stored for this imminent war. The war did not come, but they waited, expectantly, for a long time. Or maybe the war did come and they were blissfully unaware of it?

Just the other day, when her madam had had contractors to dig out the garage floor, she had called Katy and explained what they were doing. "You see, we are going to make a shelter here," she said. "Just in case. And we are stockpiling."

On seeing Katy's confused frown, her madam had explained what stockpiling was. Immediately, she knew that if her madam was right, she and almost all her neighbours in Lavender Hill would suffer, as there was no money to stockpile. There was not enough money to meet everyday expenses, where still to provide for the future? Mrs Lackay next door, for instance, had had a new baby and they did not have electricity, not because they did not pay for it, but because they did not have the money to pay the water account that went back a few years. It is no joke to struggle without electricity when you have a small baby. And winter was coming. It was already the first week of April.

Katy shook her head to rid herself of these depressing thoughts. She went about her business of helping her madam to clear the cupboards – kitchen cupboards, hall cupboards, the cupboards in the spare bedroom, and packing away boxes of tinned meats, tinned beans, packets of candles and packets of matches, boxes of powdered soups and cooking oil, sugar, tea, rice, she could go on forever. What really amused her were the few Beatrice stoves and the drum of paraffin. What would her madam do if the need for these things did not arise after all? Katy knew! One day, some years into the future, her madam will call her and tell her she can take the Beatrice stoves for herself, not failing to tell her that they were still brand new. And what will *she* do with them? Probably give them away to someone who can use them. Maybe through the church.

Her madam told her that all the white people she knew were stockpiling and she was sure some of the coloured people were doing it too. She had thought about it briefly then, and decided that she would simply hope that it would not be necessary. Hope, that was all her pocket could afford, and maybe a packet of candles. No, never mind the candles. She always had candles in the house in any case. One never knew when the lights would fail, one had to be prepared.

Katy sighed, sweeping up a little mound of sugar that had escaped from a torn packet. Her thoughts drifted back to her own mother's circumstances so long ago. They were similar to hers now, but there was a difference. Yes, her father was jobless too, but not because he couldn't get a job. He chose not to work. Her own husband, Hennie, walked to the robots every day where everyone looking for odd jobs sat around, and mostly had no luck. Every morning, he put on an overall and took a parcel of sandwiches with him, so much he tried to believe he would be hired, but as he said, you have to push your way through the crowd and jump onto the backs of bakkies and trucks before they stop. That was nearly impossible. He was a small man and timid. No, she could not see her Hennie pushing people out of the way. So, every day he returned home, his face more drawn and unsmiling than the day before.

45

"Even if you must make a loan somewhere to buy provisions," her madam was saying, "it is necessary. Think about your kids."

A loan. And how was she supposed to pay it back? She thought about it for a while as she repacked a cupboard, squeezing in tins of tuna where she could manage.

She could, of course, borrow from her mother. But no, she would not have it. She would not accept a cent that was tainted with other people's suffering. Her mother was living in Hanover Park with four guards. An old grey-haired woman with four skollies to guard her. The truth is that she had her own shebeen. It was wrong. Liquor destroys lives. How could her mother do that? After all, was it not liquor that destroyed her mother's marriage? That finally killed her father?

He looked so pathetic lying there all swollen up, in a pink hospital nightgown. She stayed at his bedside until he died. He asked her to fetch him some water and when she returned he was gone, just like that. Strangely, she felt nothing. Just thought to herself that her mother could at least also have come to the hospital to . . . to say goodbye?

After the death of her father, she saw even less of her mother. At first she did not believe what people were saying about her mother, but then one Sunday she took a bus to Hanover Park to investigate. She did not like what she saw. It was mid-afternoon and her mother was still lying in bed. Her grey hair was straggly, her nightgown was discoloured and did little to hide her shrivelled breasts. Her false teeth were in a jar of water on the sideboard next to the bed. The bed was in the front room right next to the front door. There was also a wall unit and a TV set, very nice, mind you. Through a filthy lace curtain Katie noticed that the actual bedroom was used as a store-room, piled high with crates of wine flagons.

Her mother was surprised to see her and the guards wanted to know who she was and respected her when told that she was the long-lost daughter "wat te besig is om vir haar ma te kom kyk". They brought her a chair to sit on, but she refused to sit, of course.

The place was noisy and crowded. People – sometimes even children – came to the door with empty bottles of all sorts and sizes which one of the guards filled with cheap wine from a flagon.

She had told her mother in no uncertain terms that she disagreed with her lifestyle, that it was against the will of God, but her mother sighed and said that after Mrs Fowles had died, she found it difficult to get a job, only a few chars a week and that would not have paid for the rent, let alone buy food. And there was some mistake on her birth certificate so she could not get a state pension yet. Besides, the money was good and her health was slowing down so she no longer had the strength nor energy to go down on her knees to clean floors and things like that.

Katy wondered how her mother was now. Probably alright, she reassured herself. Or else, she would have heard from someone.

"You know, Katy," her madam interrupted her thoughts, "you do not realise the seriousness of things. We would have sold the house and gone back to England if we could. They say there's going to be chaos during the elections, and after that there's worse to come."

Her madam stood up from the floor and stretched. Her willowy frame reminded Katy of a blade of grass in the breeze, fragile, but not affected.

"Of course, there are many K's willing to pay for houses here," her madam said thoughtfully, "but we promised the neighbours we would not do that, it would spoil the neighbourhood. And you know my husband. He is a stubborn man. He will not go back on his word. Still, I say, it's almost like we're at war already. It's every man for himself. You know, the survival of the fittest."

Katy smiled to herself. Her madam was so careful not to say certain words that might offend her, so she used initials instead – "K's" – even though Katy wasn't black herself.

"Do you have a book of life, Katy?" her madam asked her.

"Yes, Madam," she said.

"Well, then you're entitled to vote, you know," her madam said thoughtfully, adding, "if the right wing will allow the elections to go ahead. You people can also go and make your cross on the twenty-seventh. But how many understand a thing about politics? I can see the country going to ruin. Look what happened to Rhodesia and even Mozambique. Anyway, everyone is entitled to vote now. So, let's sit back and watch them mess things up."

"Yes," she said, not wishing to get involved in a conversation of this nature. In any case, no matter what anyone else said, her madam would have the last word, convinced that she was right, be it about the price of meat or the prospect of bad weather.

"I don't have anything personal against people of colour," her

47

madam was saying. "I am willing to share power. I'm willing to live next door to anyone, as long as they respect me and the neighbourhood and keep the place clean. Do you understand, Katy?"

She nodded. Did she understand?

"If you vote, Katy, who will you vote for?" her madam asked after a while, eyeing her cautiously while stirring her tea.

She had not really thought about it herself, but answered her anyway, as honestly as she could. "Mr Mandela," she said, looking her in the eye.

Somewhat abashed, her madam began stammering. "A lot of . . . *black* people won't even, you know."

"Yes," she answered out of politeness, really.

"And look at what De Klerk has done for the people," her madam argued. "He has done away with petty apartheid. He has done away with the Group Areas Act. Oh! I could go on forever!"

"Yes," she said again, getting up from her knees in front of the cupboard.

"I guess I should not have asked you that," her madam said quietly. "Your vote is your secret."

Katy walked out to the yard to fetch the towels from the line. It was a pleasant day. Clear sky, slight breeze, warm sunshine.

"Here are some more curtains for you," her madam said when she entered the house again. "I don't think I will ever use them."

Yes, there was that, the pile of curtains, linen and clothes her madam gave her every day, as they cleared cupboards for storage place for the stockpiling.

Her neighbour in Lavender Hill said she should sell the things on a fleamarket. "You'll be surprised what people buy," she said to Katy, adding, "Your Hennie can *mos* do it while he's not working. At least it will bring in a few rand. Maybe pay for the lights or something, *jy weet*."

Until then Katy had merely given the things away. She thought the fleamarket idea was not bad, but then she had to question her conscience. Was it okay to sell things that were given to you, even though you had no use for them? Even though they had been discarded?

"I suppose," her madam was saying, "I can give you an advance. I worry about you, you know."

Katy smiled.

"You just have to say so," her madam persisted.

48

"It's alright," she answered quietly.

"What's alright, Katy?" her madam asked agitatedly. "Do you want the money or not?"

"No," she said, taken aback. "No, I say it's alright."

"I don't understand you people," her madam said later when Katy was about to leave for home. "I offer to help you and you don't want it. Don't come crying to me when it's too late."

She wondered if she was just being stubborn, as she walked down the road to find a taxi. The taxis were full and she was tired, but something caught her eye. It was the slogan at the back of a passing taxi – *Your vote is your voice.*

That said it all. Suddenly she understood. She was a real South African now. She never had a voice before. Her mother never had a voice before. Her father never had a voice. Her vote was her voice. The "your" in the slogan meant *her*, Katy Hendricks.

She would speak to her neighbours and they would go together. Maybe they should go early, before seven, when the voting stations open. Someone said that the school opposite their block was a voting station. Yes, they must go. And they would each carefully make a cross in the appropriate block. And afterwards they could come home and have tea in her house. Maybe she'll make some scones – if there is enough flour in the house. After all, the twenty-seventh was going to be a public holiday.

Dianne Case was born in Woodstock, Cape Town, the eldest of four children. The family later moved to a big old house in Wynberg, where she spent most of her childhood playing in the huge garden with her sister Gail. Her mother read them stories most evenings. At eight years Dianne was writing her own stories. She has had three novels for teenagers published – all award winners of the MML Young Africa Award – *Albatross winter*, *Love, David* and *92 Queens Road*, which also received the 1991 Percy Fitzpatrick Award. The last two books have also been published in the United States. Most recently she published four Afrikaans *Ster-stories* for Sub A's. Before turning to full-time writing at the end of 1994, she was an office administrator.

Marita van der Vyver

St Christopher on the Parade

People, people, people. Hordes of people all around me. Music too – a drum beat and singing from a stage – but scarcely audible above the hubbub of people.

And everyone is waiting. You can almost grab hold of the anticipation. It hangs over us like a heavy blanket, a blanket that makes us sweat in the sunshine, such excited anticipation. Perhaps even claustrophobic. Like, *I can't breathe*. Because too many of us are standing too close together, because there isn't enough air for all our lungs, because one can easily be trampled today.

Or am I the only one thinking like this? Because I'm white and not accustomed to crowds? Always enjoyed enough space, my own bed in my own bedroom, a big house with a passage and a garden with a willow tree. My brother loved climbing in it. My brother . . .

When I arrived here two hours ago, I could still raise my elbows on either side of my body. Near me, a group of young women danced in a circle, clapping their hands and giggle-giggle-giggling so happily I wished I could join them. I could understand snatches of their song, odd words that Beauty has taught us over the years while she ironed our clothes, but not enough. I've never really understood enough.

But now, no one can dance any more, just sway to the beat of the music we can barely make out. To my left stands a black man, perspiring in his black suit, shame, he must feel even hotter than I do, and beside him, three brown men in overalls and beside them a couple of white girls in weird outfits – probably UCT students. A little way ahead a small blond boy sits on his father's shoulders. And to my right stands an elderly Malay woman with a white headscarf, and before her a plump little girl in a pink party dress, all frills and bows, with a huge pink bow like a giant butterfly that has landed on her head. All she can see are the legs of the people around her.

I can't help it, I can't stand crowds. My excuse has always been the time I got lost at Newlands, the day my brother let go of my hand. It was just after a big rugby match, there were thousands of people all in a hurry to get home – and suddenly I was alone. Four years old and terrifyingly alone in a sea of people.

My stomach still feels hollow when I think about it.

He hadn't let go of my hand, Darius insisted afterwards: I pulled away. But *he* got the hiding, after my father tracked me down to the police station.

Since that day I have been terrified of being trapped in a crowd, and yet here I am, voluntarily, pressed in amongst thousands of strangers. I must be crazy.

But four years ago my brother wanted to be here. And four years ago I wanted to come with him, but Mum wouldn't hear of it. No, Kitta, put it out of your mind, it's too dangerous . . .

Then.

The child with the pink butterfly on her head starts crying, some-one has trodden on her foot. I ask the Malay woman if I can put her up on my shoulders, like the little blond boy on his father's shoulders.

"Thank you, lovey!" The woman's face breaks open in a smile of gratitude. She is slightly built, and her white headscarf barely reaches my shoulder. "I'm too old. She's too heavy for me."

For me too. That is my first thought as I pick her up. Heavier than your backpack when you set off for a couple of days' hiking in the mountains. Worse than a backpack because a backpack doesn't try to throttle you. Her name is Rehana, the woman tells me, and she's four. My name is Kitta, I want to say, but Rehana's arms are so tightly clasped around my neck that I can only gurgle.

"Look, Granny," says Rehana. "Look, I can see!"

Four years can make a big difference. Not just in a country, but also in a life. Four years ago I was a fourteen-year-old schoolgirl with legs like a secretary bird's, a brace on my teeth and a pimply fore-head. Now I'm a student and I don't need my mother's permission to be here.

Like millions of other South Africans, I voted for the first time just the other day – 27 April 1994. Before that, I simply hadn't been the right age, not the wrong skin colour as well, but it was still a bonus to vote for the first time on such a historic day. For the first time I felt as though I belonged here, on this continent, in this country, right here where I'm standing today.

Four years ago, when Nelson Mandela was released from prison, my brother wanted to be here for his first speech. At the time he was the same age as I am now, fresh out of school, on his way to medical school. Much cleverer than me, the brainiest in our school.

That was before our school was "opened". All the children used to be white. They are still almost all white – just a dark face here and there, like a chocolate chip in a bowl of vanilla ice-cream – because "good" schools in "good" neighbourhoods don't change colour overnight. As the head reassured our anxious parents. But Darius had made friends with Beauty's son and started asking questions that irritated Dad. (Or did he start asking the questions first and make friends with Percy afterwards?) We all know Percy. Sometimes of a weekend he'd wash Dad's car or mow the lawn, but one day Darius stopped calling him Percy and started referring to him as Sipho. They talked for hours about jazz and reggae and rap, and Percy took Darius to the township. When Darius came back, he asked Mum whether she'd ever been to see the "desperate conditions" in which people were living there. Mum nearly had a fit when she discovered where he'd been. And that he'd gone there in a minibus-taxi. After that he never told her if he'd been to see Percy. Sipho.

When my brother heard that Nelson Mandela was to be released, he leaped up and down as if he was watching a rugby match, yelling, "Yes, yes, yes! Viva! Amandla!" – that sort of thing. Dilly with excitement. He said he was going to drink himself into a stupor to celebrate the birth of democracy.

Then.

But now it feels as though I'm carrying a backpack full of hot coals. My shoulders are on fire and the flames are licking at my neck. Me and my big mouth. If I'd known the child was so heavy, if I'd known we'd have to wait so long, I'd never have offered to pick her up. I thought the wait was nearly over. It should have been over by now. African time! That's what Dad always says. With a sigh.

"Shame, lovey," says the child's grandmother when she hears my sigh. "*Sy's swaar, nè? Wil jy dalk 'n lemoen hê?*"

I suck the orange gratefully, grateful for the sweetness, the juiciness, grateful that the woman is speaking to me in Afrikaans. I feel as if I'd passed a test.

"It's for her sake that I'm here," explains the woman, still in Afrikaans, her eyes little black slits against the sun as she looks up at me. Her face isn't brown, I realise, it is the colour of caramelised condensed milk. The deep lines under her eyes gleam with moisture. "So that one day she can tell her grandchildren that she was here. That her granny brought her."

"I came for the sake of my brother," I say. "He wanted to be here when Mandela was released, but he was killed a couple of days earlier. In a motor accident."

"Shame, lovey," she says, squeezing my arm.

I blink back the tears. Am I mad to stand here telling something like this to a complete stranger?

At precisely this moment something happens to the crowd. The blanket of expectation turns into an electric blanket. It feels like when you get back into your warm bed after going to the bathroom on a cold night, like a delicious slow-creeping goose flesh. Nelson Mandela has arrived at the City Hall. He is going to appear on the balcony and address the sea of people on the Parade.

And the sea begins rumbling in advance. We cheer. All of us. Me too. Through the tears. Oh, God, I miss my brother. And I hear the high, clear laughter of a child somewhere over my head.

And I realise, amazed, that I no longer feel the weight upon my shoulders.   *C. K.*

Born in Cape Town, Marita van der Vyver attended schools in Cape Town, Pretoria and Nelspruit. In matric she won first prize in a national poetry competition: a bursary for four years of university study in Afrikaans. She went to Stellenbosch, where she later received an M.A. in Journalism. She is an acclaimed juvenile writer (*Van jou Jas, Tien vir 'n vriend, Eenkantkind*), co-author of a biography of the political activist Anton Lubowski (*Paradox of a man*), and she won various literary prizes for her first adult novel *Griet skryf 'n sprokie*, which has appeared in translation in several foreign languages. Her latest novel is *Die dinge van 'n kind.* When not writing fiction, Marita works as freelance journalist and columnist.

Lesley Beake

The new beginning

We couldn't believe it when the elections were over. The fighting had stopped. Everything was quiet. People were scared to be happy at first. Was it really over? Was the fighting finished? Ma said seeing was believing and *she* wasn't going to start celebrating too soon, but Aunty got out a bottle of sweet wine and said we should make a toast to the New South Africa.

Hendrik came round from next door. Nobody notices that Hendrik is white any more. We've all got used to having him around. Hendrik said his ma sent her best wishes. He didn't say anything about his pa. Hendrik's pa is not so happy about the New South Africa, but Hendrik says that's *his* problem. Hendrik says the old people might need a bit longer to get used to the idea, but he's glad he doesn't have to see all that killing on television any more.

Aunty said we should all stand up, which we did. Then she lifted her glass high up, so that the light shone through it, red like rubies. .''To the future!'' she shouted, and we all clinked our glases so that the sticky sweet stuff ran down over our fingers, and we laughed and drank and hoped in our hearts that it really *was* real, even Ma.

Aunty gave Hendrik and me another glass when Ma wasn't looking. "Haai!" she said, winking at Hendrik, "here's to a better future, man!" Hendrik looked pleased. Hendrik doesn't get to go to many parties. His pa doesn't like it. Hendrik's pa is a pain.

So the next week Ma, Aunty, and I went to the Grand Parade in Cape Town to see the proper beginning when Mr Mandela came to talk to the people after he had been to Parliament for the first time.

Hendrik wanted to come, but his ma wouldn't let him. She said the right-wingers might make trouble. Funny that, how everybody was suddenly scared of violence from the white people.

Old Mrs Donald, who Ma works for, said she was too old to go and stand in a crowd in the sun. She said that she would be there in spirit and would be watching everything on her television. Mrs Donald was in the Black Sash for about a hundred years, so she feels she is part of what is happening now. "When I was younger," Mrs Donald says, "we had to keep believing that someday things would change for the better – and now they have!" Mrs Donald hasn't stopped smiling since the first day of the elections.

Ma had quite a lot of trouble with Aunty who wanted to wear a special outfit in the ANC colours, and a big hat. Ma said people wouldn't be able to see past the hat, and she thought Aunty had always been a DP supporter. Aunty said the New South Africa was all about change, so she was as well, but she saw the point about the hat and also about not wearing her high heels. Ma said it would be just like standing at the crayfish factory all day, only with more to watch.

We got there early. It was a bit scary at first because there were more policemen than there were people. They were standing all along the streets that led to the Parade. At first I thought they looked angry, but then I thought that maybe they were scared. If there was trouble, they were going to be in it. I saw some of the young ones sharing a packet of fruit drops, and looking afraid. I smiled at them, and one of them smiled back, but he didn't offer me a fruit drop.

Ma chose us a place on the Parade where we had a palm tree behind us – in case the crowd pushed, she said. We couldn't see the bands that played for the people, which made Aunty a bit cross, but Ma said we had come to see our President, not a crowd of musicians, and anyway we could hear them loud enough – loud enough even for Aunty.

All morning the people came and came. Some of them came in groups, running and toyi-toyi-ing and waving flags. Old people came, and people with small babies. Many young people came, and their faces were glad. White people came – some of them also wearing ANC colours. I wondered if they had also changed for the New South Africa, or if we just hadn't known about them before.

Behind us was an old, old Xhosa man who stood quiet and glad, looking and looking towards the balcony of the City Hall where Mr Mandela would come out to speak. Ma offered him a cheese sandwich, but he didn't want one. "Today I need no food," he said, "today I have too much joy to feel hunger."

"Shame," Aunty said, "shame, the old toppie looks as if he could do with something to eat later." She made him put a sandwich wrapped in tin foil in his pocket. "We'd better have *our* cheese sandwiches while we can still lift our hands to our mouths!" she said.

The crowd was pushing like Ma had said. It was a good thing that we did eat right then because after that there was a heavy push from behind as more and more and more people came to the Parade to see our new President. The crowd clapped and waved and sang with the music of the bands. It was very hot. And then, just when there was no more room for another person on the Grand Parade, we heard that Mr Mandela had arrived at the back door of the City Hall.

I will never forget that time. The crowd was so tight around me that we felt like one person, breathing together, and feeling together.

"A pity Hendrik's not here," Aunty said. "Stupid old ma he's got. Do *you* see any right-wingers?" she whispered to me. I said no, but I didn't look because a whole lot of people came out onto the balcony – ladies in hats, men in dark suits – and we cheered them all, waving our hands, swaying together and shouting.

Mr De Klerk came out and there was a special cheer for him. Bishop Tutu came out. I've never seen anybody look as happy as Bishop Tutu did that day! He looked like he was going to bounce right over the edge of the balcony with happiness, like a purple bouncing ball. There were some speeches, but I didn't listen to them much. The people cheered Mr De Klerk a lot when he spoke, but we were all just waiting, really. And then Bishop Tutu told us the President was coming and I felt the noise of the people coming up from the ground as they shouted, "Amandla! Viva! Long Live!"

"Amandla! Viva! Long Live!"

It was like the sea in a great storm, that noise. It rushed past me and up and out into the great blue sky that was over us, and my heart flew with it. It joined with all the other voices and hearts on that whole Grand Parade, and it was the best thing that had ever happened to me. I hoped Hendrik was watching all of this on their television. And old Mrs Donald.

Then Mr Mandela came slowly forward, waving and smiling; listening to us, listening to the sound of the people of South Africa saying welcome, saying welcome back, saying thank you for what he did.

When Mr Mandela spoke, every ear listened. He told us in that careful way he has that it was true. The New South Africa had really come. We could really believe it. We were free!

After that, when we sang, I cried. Lots of people were crying and everybody was holding their hands high in the Peace Sign. All around me was warmth and smiling and happiness. In that moment we were one voice, and one heart.

We *are* one people at last:

Nkosi sikelel' iAfrika
Maluphakayisw' uphondo lwayo
Yiva nemithandazo yethu
Nkosi sikelela, Nkosi sikelela

Nkosi sikelel' iAfrika
Maluphakayisw' uphondo lwayo
Yiva nemithandazo yethu
Nkosi sikelela, thina lusapho lwayo

Yihla moya, Yihla moya, Yihla
Yihla moya, Yihla moya, Yihla
Yihla, moya, oyingcwele
Thina lusapho lwayo

Morena bolokwa sechaba sa hesa
Ofedise dintwa lematshwenyeho

O se boloke, o se boloke
O se boloke, o se boloke
Sechaba sa heso
Sechaba sa heso

O se boloke, o se boloke
O se boloke, o se boloke
Sechaba sa heso
Sechaba sa Afrika

Lesley Beake was born and went to school in Edinburgh, Scotland. She studied at Rhodes University and through UNISA, and has lived and travelled extensively in Africa and the Middle East. She writes for children of all ages. Her work includes twenty books, published in nine different countries and six different languages. Her many awards include the MML Young Africa Award, the Percy Fitzpatrick Award for *The strollers* and *Cage full of butterflies*, which was also awarded the M-Net Book Prize. Her young adult novel *Song of Be* was elected Children's Book of Note for 1993 by the American Library Association. She also writes for magazines and radio.

Lawrence Bransby

A reflection of self

Victor awoke with a faint but discernible sense of well-being beneath his tiredness. He savoured it, as if tasting a sweet: it wasn't as strong as euphoria, but there was very definitely a something, a satisfaction which he could feel within his breast.

He allowed his mind to search for the cause: a compliment, perhaps? a present unopened? a girl?

His thoughts were interrupted by a brief knock at the door and his father, pyjamaed, bespectacled and unshaven, entered bearing a cup of tea in both hands as he attempted a grotesque toyi-toyi. "Welcome, son of mine, to the New South Africa!" he cried, spilling tea on his arm.

The New South Africa – *that* was it!

Victor grinned and rubbed his eyes. "Thanks, Dad!"

He found it interesting that it had affected him so deeply, this new era in the history of his country, that it had been absorbed into his sub-conscious so that he could wake feeling as he did.

They – his father, mother and Victor – had sat up in front of the television the night before, watching the ceremony as the old South African flag was lowered at midnight and the new flag with its brightly coloured "Y" was raised, the strains of "Nkosi sikelel' iAfrica" drowned by the cheering of ecstatic crowds.

His mother and father had reminisced into the early hours, looking back over the apartheid years. Now, the next morning, his father grinned as he sat on the side of Victor's bed. The springs complained and Victor had to wriggle over to keep upright. He leaned on his elbow and sipped his tea.

"I was thinking, you know, this morning –" his father began.

"Amazing –" Victor mocked.

His father laughed. "No, seriously –"

Victor valued his relationship with his father. Ever since he could remember, his father had treated him as an equal, had shared his innermost thoughts with him, had tried to lead Victor towards being the thinking human being he expected him to be – in essence, a re-flection of what he felt himself to be.

"It struck me, you know," his father continued, sombre now, "that, although I've been a South African all my life – born here, ancestors here since 1820 – only today, now, these last few hours, have I at last attained spiritual citizenship of my country. It was a profound thought . . ."

"I know," Victor said, understanding. "It's like –" he searched for an image, "forgiveness, isn't it? Then starting again . . ."

Victor recalled his parents' reminiscences of the previous night, how long ago they had been labelled "liberal" by most of their friends, a term of slight opprobrium, usually spoken with a subtle curl of the lip. They had been "Progs", members of the Progressive Party which, to most whites, was a little too progressive, smacking of communism in its advocation of equality with blacks.

Sipping dark red wine, they told (as they had many times before) how during their student days they had done the obligatory protest-ing against the Nat regime, waving placards and chanting in front of the stone lion of the cenotaph in Gardner Street.

But most students did that. It's what students do, Victor thought. They even pasted THIS IS PETTY APARTHEID stickers on WHITES ONLY signs outside toilets and on benches in the city centre. This was done at night, of course, and it was rather fun. But in a small way, they were striking a blow.

They talked on, smug in a way that events had proved them right. But in the early hours Victor realised with a shock that his parents were doing more than reminiscing; there was a hollowness in their voices, and in their eyes, which cried: but was what we did really enough . . .?

Victor's father was a teacher of English and in a way had been persecuted for his liberal stand, denied promotion (he was sure), la-belled a kaffir-boetie. He never really spoke politics in the classroom – "That wasn't allowed; one could be fired for that," he said, perhaps a little too vehemently.

But he would (when the moment was opportune) make a point within the context of a lesson, and if the point happened to be politi-cal, racial or social in nature, then so be it. His conscience dictated that he make *some* stand against what he knew was an immoral and untenable social order.

It was his duty, he said.

Once he was briefly investigated by the Special Branch for using a satirical political cartoon in an exercise on emotive language. Victor realised that it made his father proud in a way. If the Special Branch were interested in him then he *had* to be doing something constructive (or destructive, depending on how you looked at it!) against apartheid, chipping away at the block, however small.

Victor too had thought often about these things. He found it difficult to believe that benches had actually had WHITES ONLY signs attached to them; that blacks had had to sit at the backs of buses. How could his parents have *lived* through it all, accepted it, done so little?

When he was a child Victor had not even been aware that things were different for other children, that all the patrons at the fun fair which came every July to Durban and filled his night with its lights and smells and sounds were white. His parents had expressed their outrage and shown him the picture in the *Daily News* of a sad little black face looking through the railings at the excitement reserved for white children only; but he hadn't really understood. Perhaps they should have refused to take him there – as a protest, Victor thought.

And then, by the time Victor became aware, most of the petty structures of apartheid had already been torn down. He was therefore denied the opportunity of doing anything about those . . .

Victor convinced himself that had he been old enough during those times, he would have done something about it – some grand gesture, perhaps been arrested, his photo on the front page of the *Sunday Tribune*: "TEENAGER ARRESTED FOR FLOUTING SEPARATE AMENITIES ACT . . . 'It was the least I could do,' Matthews said when interviewed from his cell while awaiting trial . . ."

His father had even done National Service. "In those days you just *did*," he admitted, and Victor could sense his embarrassment.

Victor wished *he* could refuse to do his National Service like Charles Bester and other young men who had gone to prison for their moral stand. He pictured himself before the judge: "Your Honour, apartheid is an abomination in the sight of humanity and God. I cannot in all good conscience . . ." and the judge's words rang out: "Victor Matthews, I have no alternative but to sentence you to six years' imprisonment without the option of a fine . . ."

The time for grand gestures against apartheid seemed to be over. Victor felt cheated.

Well, he thought, he *had* suffered the abuse of his friends when he tried to take a stand on the equality of all people; or tried to counter with logic the often repeated racist anecdotes, told with such relish.

He had made a point not to call their maid "the girl" or refer to Samuel (who worked in the garden each Saturday) as "the garden boy". He always called them by their names, accorded them that dignity.

He had even tried to learn a few words of Zulu. There had been a programme on television a few years before.

For all that, the change had occurred: Apartheid was dead, the New South Africa had dawned and he felt good.

His father, perched like a gaunt bird on the edge of his bed, was saying, ". . . look him in the eye like a brother. It's as if a huge cloud of guilt has been lifted, you know?"

"Yes," Victor said, "I know. The white man's guilt as opposed to the white man's burden . . ."

His father laughed, a sharp bark of sound.

After a late breakfast, followed almost immediately by the traditional 10 o'clock cup of coffee, Victor's mother asked him to be a good boy and go to the café to buy rolls for lunch. He went eagerly, glad to clear his head of sleep and coffee.

Outside, the street was warm but touched with the first hint of autumn chill. The first person Victor came across was a black man leaning against the STOP pole at the street corner. Victor saw him with new eyes: he was an equal, a fellow South African, a person; Victor suppressed a desire to walk up to this leaning black man, shake his hand, call him Brother. He wanted so badly to tell him of his new perspective, his changed view. Drawn by Victor's stare, the man turned. Their eyes met and the man smiled. To Victor it was a smile from one man to another. It filled him with a strange sense of joy.

Outside the café a group of people stood, talking Zulu. Victor wanted to go to them and say, "I'm a South African now! So are you! We're *real* at last!" but he didn't. When they watched him as he entered the door of the dingy café, he didn't feel the brooding resentment his white skin had often evoked in the past. It didn't seem to matter any more.

Could things really have changed so much in such a short time? Victor wondered. He was filled with hope and anticipation for the future.

The café was crowded; over the babble of voices, a radio played determinedly. The air was thick with smells of body odour, as well as fresh bread, pink sweets, samoosas and pies in the warming oven, fresh fruit and vegetables.

Victor jostled through to the baskets of fresh rolls and counted a dozen into two plastic bags, tying the ends carefully so that they wouldn't split.

At the till, the queue was fairly long. It wasn't a queue, exactly, more a bustle of bodies; except for him, all were black. He stood, easing himself between spaces as they opened.

The man at the till was Greek, or Portuguese – Victor didn't really know, something like that. He and his wife and their black-eyed, black-haired daughter lived in a flat above the shop and spoke a foreign language whenever they communicated with each other. Victor knew them, but not by name.

He moved slowly forwards, pressed on all sides by bodies; ahead of him, at the till, a woman with a black *doek* covering her head was having difficulty extracting her purse from her bra; behind her was an old bent woman and immediately in front of Victor was a man with his brown head shaved bald, the folds of his neck constricted by a frayed collar.

The man at the till glanced up and, recognising Victor across the space which separated them, he smiled. Victor smiled back, happy and at peace with the world.

As soon as the store owner had handed the woman with the *doek* her change, he half stood and reached his hand over the press of bodies, favouring Victor as had often happened in the past when a white stood in line behind blacks.

Without thinking, Victor lifted the bags over the shoulder of the man in front of him while he felt in his pocket for his money.

And it was then, as the shop owner took the money from his hand, as the man with the frayed collar turned to look him in the face, sharing the wordless reproach of the old woman now waiting at the till, that Victor realised what he had done.

For a moment, he saw as they saw.

He turned away confusedly, leaving his change, leaving the rolls, pushing through the bodies which seemed to close him in.

In front of his eyes the worn green and black Marley tiles with their flattened cigarette butts and a striped Chappie's paper blurred as he stumbled towards the door, past the sullen eyes which watched him, and into the street . . .

Lawrence Bransby, at present Deputy Principal of Ixopo High in the Natal Midlands, was born in Umhlanga Rocks in 1951. He matriculated from Beachwood High in Durban and attended the universities of Natal in Durban and Western Australia in Perth, where he obtained a B.Ed. degree. Lawrence has had five novels for teenagers published: *Down Street*, winner of the MER Prize; *Homeward bound*, runner-up for the M-Net Book Prize; *Remember the whales*, winner of the Volkskas Bank Prize; *The geek in shining armour* and *A mountaintop experience*. A novel for adults with the theme of conscientious objection is with an agent in London at the moment, and two further teenage novels are with publishers. This is the first short story he has ever attempted.

Barrie Hough

The journey

"Why don't you stammer when you shout?" Thembi asked him as they sat on the bench under the delicately flowering pepper tree. Johan's lips brushed against the thin beaded braids as she turned her head away from him.

"I refuse to kiss a boy who stutters. And do we really want to spoil a lovely friendship by complicating it?" He could see, from the way her lips twitched, that she was trying hard not to smile.

"B-b-but that's d-discrimination," he laughed. And yet he clenched his fists so that the nails cut into his palms. "I also don't st-stammer when I sing."

"Life's not a musical. When you are able to whisper to me without stammering, whisper sweet nothings, then you can kiss me." Thembi opened his fist and squeezed his hand gently.

The bell rang.

During Maths he imagined he could still catch the sweet scent of her braids. But her cruelty cut into his heart. He failed to understand it.

Despite her initial mistrust, Johan had been warm and friendly to her ever since she arrived at the school. Her parents lived far away and she was a boarder. He sensed her loneliness. He asked his parents to invite her to Sunday lunch. Thembi and his mother had hit it off well and she became a regular visitor.

At school Johan had kept his ear to the ground. Nobody really said offensive things to her. But the expression in their eyes wounded more than words would have. Early on in life, Johan had learnt to read this "quiet" language – from the time he knew that his speech was different to that of other children.

His understanding of this language drew him close to Thembi and made him feel protective towards her. Not that she had ever really needed protection. She was cheeky and sharp and soon became chairperson of the debating society. Although her Afrikaans pronunciation was sometimes strange, her English was perfect. And when some-

one made her really angry, she let off steam in Setswana, which few
pupils at the school understood.

Thembi was clever, especially in Science and Biology. She wanted
to be a doctor, like her father. She wanted to *do* things, make a difference. Politicians were a breed she disliked. "They're word pedlars,"
she scoffed. "And words are cheap. Politicians use them to pull the
wool over people's eyes."

Yet Johan had caught her out on the day of President Mandela's
inauguration. He, Thembi and a few other friends had watched TV
at his parents' house. Thembi had joined the group in hooting with
laughter at the strange fashions and headdresses the VIP guests had
sported. Marike de Klerk, they agreed, looked a little like Meryl
Streep in *Out of Africa* and everybody wondered why the president's
daughter hid under such a big hat.

Johan had joined the chorus of gentle mockery but various
speakers caught his attention. They speak so fluently, their words
pour like cream from a jug, he had thought. These commentators and
the imbongi who gushes in a singing tone.

When *Die Stem* and *Nkosi Sikelel' iAfrika* were played and the
cannon salute sounded while President Mandela held his hand
against his chest, Johan had glanced at Thembi and saw her wipe
away some tears. He had nudged her. "I thought they were all w-
word pedlars."

"Suka!" she had said with a sweeping gesture of her hand. Later
her only defence had been, "You also shed a tear, Boertjie."

The second last period was English. While Miss Cooke explained
to the class how timeless Shakespeare was and how the musical *West
Side Story* was *Romeo and Juliet* in a contemporary setting, a note
landed on Johan's desk.

> See you on the rugby field after school.
>   Thembi xxx

Johan tried to catch her eye but she was listening intently to Miss
Cooke. He couldn't speak to her during the last period either.

But when he got to the rugby field, Thembi was waiting for him.
"If you can shout without a stammer, you should also be able to
speak and whisper fluently," she said. "I have a plan. You go to one
set of goal posts, I go to the other. We walk slowly towards each

other. At first you'll have to shout so that I can hear you. Then, as you approach me, you tone down until you speak, and eventually whisper."

Johan exploded. "You can all go jump in the bloody lake!" he shouted. "I've been trying for years. Speech therapists and shrinks since I've been *this* high. On the phone I struggle. Orals are a n-nightmare. In primary school the kids used to laugh at me. Always looked at me as though I was a moron. Everybody in the family always gave advice. 'Give him a good *skrik*. Put pebbles in his mouth. Make him sing.' I've had it, do you hear! I've had it. And now *you!*"

He saw Thembi extending her hand towards him. But she hesitated and said softly, "Do you really think I don't understand, that I don't know how it feels?" She turned and walked away.

When she was through the gate and had disappeared around the corner, Johan roared and hurled stones at the posts.

The following day it was Johan's turn to send a note.

After school Thembi waited on the rugby field.

In the weeks that followed, Johan's voice was frequently hoarse. Only he and Thembi knew the reason.

When the pepper tree flourished its red berries, they no longer started at opposite ends of the field. Johan no longer shouted. He merely spoke loudly. Occasionally, when he grew too excited about his progress, he stumbled over his words. Then Thembi would stop him. And sometimes he lost heart because the journey took so long.

And then, one afternoon, shortly before the end of term, they had moved so close to one another that Johan had to whisper.

He stood still. She could smell the peppermint on his breath. They smiled and both burst out laughing. They ran around with their arms in the air. He shouted, she ululated.

When they were tired, he walked up to her. Out of breath, he whispered. He leaned towards her. She did not turn her head away again.

Barrie Hough, a born and bred Johannesburger, is an arts journalist, columnist and arts editor of *Rapport*. After completing an M.A. in English on Athol Fugard's work, at the Rand Afrikaans University, he taught Afrikaans at St Barnabas College in Johannesburg. He left teaching for journalism and was theatre critic at *Beeld* until 1987, when he moved to *Rapport*. His first novel for young people, *My kat word herfs*, appeared in 1986. His second, *Droomwa*, received the 1990 Sanlam Silver Prize for Youth Literature. In 1992 his *Vlerkdans* garnered Gold in the same competition. Other awards include the AA Vita Award for Theatre Journalism, the Alba Bouwer Prize, the C.P. Hoogenhout Medal and the ATKV Children's Book Award. All three his juvenile novels have been translated into English.

Dianne Hofmeyr

The magic man

Why the dove chose her windowsill, she was never sure but when it settled there for the third time, she knew it was some sort of sign.

Down below on the pavement the magic man smiled up at her and waved but she didn't open the window nor did she wave back. From behind the glass, she watched the dove as it flew down again. A group of children, tugging at the magic man and demanding more tricks, flustered the bird so that it fluttered around before resettling on his shoulder.

From where she stood next to the curtain she'd seen how the magic man had slipped the dove from his pocket and hidden it inside his hat before putting it back on his head. And she had seen the children look startled when he removed the hat and the white dove was sitting on the top of his head, looking as if it had hatched there. She'd seen how he'd manipulated his hands so that a chocolate came out miraculously from behind a little girl's ear and a sucker appeared mysteriously on a boy's shoulder. She'd seen how he'd popped some hankies into his mouth and how they'd come out from his sleeve knotted together magically in a string.

She knew his tricks.

But down on the pavement, still mystified, the children giggled and laughed and demanded more.

When the magic man looked up unexpectedly again and smiled at her, she was caught unawares and guiltily dropped the curtain.

From then onwards he came to the same place on the pavement every day. She didn't have to go to the window to know he was there. She would see the dove on her windowsill and she'd hear the children laughing. Then one day there were footsteps on the stairs. Not the slow sounds of someone coming home from work, but great energetic thumps as if the person was taking the stairs three at a time. Then there was rapid knocking on her door and her heart seemed to thump just as loudly against her ribs.

In the seven weeks that she'd lived in the block of flats no one had ever knocked on her door. The sound was so startling that she sat and stared at the colours of the chipped paint around the handle of the chain lock. The baby started to cry and the person on the other side of the door seemed to knock more enthusiastically.

When she opened it a crack, it was him, the magic man from down on the pavement. In his hand he held a flower that he offered to her in the same way that he held out a sucker for the children. When she didn't take it, he laid it at her feet and turned and left. Afterwards as she shushed the baby, she realised that she'd only looked into his eyes. She hadn't spoken a word and nor had he. From then onwards she left the window slightly open to listen for the sound of his voice when he made his magic down below in the afternoons.

But he never spoke.

Once when she was looking at the notice board that advertised jobs outside the Spar shop, she caught sight of him inside buying milk. Another time when she was at the laundromat staring blankly at the row of machines, he was suddenly at her side. He showed her how to make the money disappear in the slot so that the machine started magically to rumble and pump water. And once when she was taking the baby out into the park, he stopped to tickle the baby's cheek.

When he still didn't speak, she realised he was mute.

After a while he started coming up to her room regularly. And every afternoon she waited for the sound of his feet on the stairs. At first he had stood at the door with more daisies. She knew he'd picked them in the park because she had watched him from the window. Later it seemed silly to stand looking at each other across the doorway without saying anything, so she indicated that he should come in. But when she glanced around the room, seeing it as a stranger must, she realised there was nowhere for him to sit except on her bed or the floor. So she made him tea and they both sat on the floor. He showed her his hankey trick and tricks with cards and she found herself laughing like one of the children. And all the while the white dove sat on his shoulder.

Once when he pretended to chew a blade and swallow it, she knew it was hidden beneath his tongue. The sharpness of it sent a shiver through her and she couldn't stop herself. "No!" She said the word so loudly that the sound seemed to stay in the room for a long time. Then she realised it was the first word she'd ever spoken to him. Somehow his silence had made her silent.

One day he arrived at her door with an old battered suitcase and she felt her heart jump against her ribcage. She thought he was coming to say goodbye. But after they'd drunk their tea, he opened the case with a little key. One by one he took out things and handed them to her. He showed her pictures of a big circus tent and animals doing tricks. He showed her photographs of a young man wearing a sparkling red clown costume walking on a thin rope balancing a long pole across his shoulders on which doves sat while he juggled with five balls in the air. And as they passed the photographs back and forth, the magic man's hands flew over them and he pointed at what he was doing and she marvelled at the tricks.

Then he got so excited he stood up and grabbed a broom and started searching her shelf for something. When he found a box of eggs, he balanced the broom across his shoulders, flicked his fingers for the dove to sit on it and started throwing the eggs into the air and catching them in turn. She waited for him to drop one but he didn't and she laughed because she was sure that if he could have stretched a rope across the room he would have balanced on that as well.

Afterwards, from the bottom of his suitcase, he pulled out a costume. The same one that was in the photographs. Except that now it had lost many of its red sparkles. And he stroked the costume and made sounds in his throat that she didn't understand. But she watched his face and his eyes and his hands as he spoke. Then she touched the costume as well and she told him that she thought it was beautiful with or even without the sparkles.

When the baby woke, she picked it up and rocked it against her and the magic man held out his hands for the baby.

She hesitated. Then she handed it to him carefully and watched to make sure he held it properly.

She reached for a bag that had been hidden under her bed for so long now. She unzipped the bag that had kept the smell of the damp Cape mountains locked inside it. She held out the photograph of her mother standing in her pink OK Bazaars uniform and the flowered *doek* in front of the farmhouse with the farmer and his wife and the farmer's son. Then she passed him the blurred photograph of the son sitting up on the tractor, smiling into the camera as only he could smile. And the magic man held it up and looked at her and smiled as well.

Suddenly she pulled the bag wide open and turned it upside down and emptied everything she had kept in it onto the floor. While she sorted through the things, she told the magic man about them. Who had given them to her and why.

Finally she came to the tiny blue jacket and the bootees with ribbon threaded through them. She sat with her knees tucked up under her chin and she stared at them for a long time.

Then without looking up, she told him about them as well. Why she'd come to the city and why she couldn't return to the farm.

At first the words came up icy cold. So icy cold, that they almost took her breath away. Just like her breath had left her that evening when she and the farmer's son had jumped naked into the cold mountain pool. But as she brought the words closer and closer to the surface they warmed in her mouth and seemed able to spill out. She looked across into the face and the eyes of the magic man as he sat opposite her, and the frozen coldness of the words melted completely. Now she spoke until she felt there were no words left in her.

After that, she spread out all the pictures and the photographs and the red sparkling costume that had lost some of its sparkles and finally the baby clothes so that they made a complete circle around herself and the magic man and they both sat looking at them.

And then the girl knew the truth.

The truth was that the baby had died, in a pool of blood in a bucket in a tiny room somewhere in the city. And had ended up – where? Which drain? What garbage dump? She wasn't sure.

There had been no burial.

Afterwards she'd knitted the jersey and the bootees because she had hated the thought of a baby in a rough blanket only, and she had comforted him when he cried.

Now she looked at the magic man as he sat opposite her. He could not truthfully make chocolates come from children's ears, nor could he make blades disappear. Nor could he truthfully turn the empty blanket that he held against his chest into a baby again. And neither could he mend her aching heart. But she had shared her story with him and he had understood.

She reached across and took the empty blanket from him. Then she picked up the blue jersey and the bootees with ribbon threaded through them. She went to the open window. Down below on the pavement she saw the children waiting for the man to come and make magic. She leaned far out over the windowsill and held out the blanket and the clothes and let them fall from her hands. Then she watched the shapes as they floated to the pavement. She had no further use for them.

She stepped back and closed the window firmly.

 Dianne Hofmeyr was born in Somerset West. Her childhood next to the sea in Gordon's Bay has been the source of many stories, and she believes that her training as an art teacher has made her attentive to detail. Her most recent novel, *Boikie you better believe it*, won the 1994 Sanlam Gold Prize for Youth Literature. Three other novels, *When whales go free*, *A red kite in a pale sky* and *Blue train to the moon* have won the Sanlam Silver, the Sanlam Gold and the MML Young Africa Award respectively. Recently her *Do the whales still sing?*, a children's picture book illustrated by Jude Daly, was published in the United States. In 1982 Dianne moved from Stellenbosch to Johannesburg, where she is actively involved in promoting a reading culture among children and young people.

Engela van Rooyen

Your own two hands

David stirred the porridge on the smoking primus. It was he who, every morning, prepared everything in the tin shack. It was the least that he could do. He brought in no money. And he could not find a job despite having walked his feet off. There was no money to further his education even though he so desperately wanted to. He had to depend on the little money that his sister brought in and on the old people's pension.

"Would you like something to eat?" he asked Zandi, who glanced at her fingernails. She did not use nail polish. The natural look was in, she said.

She shook her head tensely. David knew there were two things bothering her. The first was that she had an interview today for a better job. The last time there was a vacancy she was away in their ancestral land to celebrate her coming of age. The old people wanted it that way. It was to be the crown on her years of submission. And when someone else got that job, Grandpa simply blamed it on the curse of Koko Sedubedube.

David knew what else was bothering Zandi because it was the same thing that was weighing heavily on his own mind. They had to tell Grandpa what they had discovered. It was a secret that they could no longer keep to themselves. Grandpa would have to hear all about Koko Sedubedube's descendant. And who could tell what would happen when Grandpa heard the truth? What David feared most was most likely to happen. He, David, would have to take revenge because Grandpa had grown too old to do so himself. He was the oldest living male member of Grandpa's descendants. And how could he convince Grandpa that revenge served no purpose? Already he was having difficulty finding a job. How much more difficult would it get if he had blood on his hands? If he got caught he would have to go to jail. If he did not get caught he would have to live with his conscience. He wanted to live for the future, a human being among human beings. He had no desire for violence.

Grandma moved her heavy body with difficulty as she picked up the tin bath. It was wash day. David knew that he would have to help.

Grandpa sat staring through the window with the small window-panes. Outside, pure white frost lay on the ground and the sand road looked like an iced cake that had fallen to pieces. That vague look in Grandpa's eyes was misleading, David thought. The old man knew about all the problems in his family, the poverty and the hard times. Only, to him it was all the fault of Koko Sedubedube. Through the years he had learnt to say this name with a dignified contempt, as if he were spitting out a sour plum, "Kokkos-doobedoobe".

It was because of Koko that Grandpa's father, Eliyasi, was forced to flee from his ancestral land all those years ago. He and his sons came here to Johannesburg to dig sewerage trenches. Poverty is something that goes on and on like a path stretching over hills. It continues among your children and their children. There is only one thing for which the old man has not blamed Koko Sedubedube, David thought: his aggressive daughter Peace, who had cast not only the two old people, but also him and Zandi, out of her home. Now Peace lived with a strange man. He was not married to Peace and this meant that Grandpa could not claim lobola from him.

"My heart is bleak," Grandpa complained to David. "The big day has arrived, but it has not come the way we all expected it to. We went to vote as we had been told to do. We stood there for hours, hunger gnawing at our bellies, the wind lashing at our faces."

"*Ewe*," said Grandma.

"One can know the veld, but never another human being," Grand-pa mumbled, but David did not understand the meaning of his words. "And a child who doesn't cry will die on its mother's back." Now David understood what he was talking about – all those things which they so desperately needed and looked forward to now that they had voted. But David also knew that what Grandpa wanted most of all was to find Koko Sedubedube's descendants.

And when he finds them . . . David pumped the primus with such intensity that it began to roar in the tiny zinc kitchen.

"There were sangomas at the inauguration," Grandpa recalled. He had watched so much TV on that day that David had to take the battery to neighbours to have it recharged. "But not one of them would know where to find Koko Sedubedube's descendants so that revenge could take its course." David sighed. His grandfather still

74

believed that they would all be able to return to their ancestral land when the injustice of the past had been avenged.

"I shall have to find my own sangoma. But where will I find goats or fowls to pay her?" Grandpa frowned.

Zandi and David exchanged sidelong glances. They never laughed at these stories. The old people were good to them. They took them in and helped them when their own mother threw them out. And then she still came at the end of every month to prey on the old people's meagre pension. She owned a shebeen, which had a bad name because there was always blood. And to crown it all her name was Peace!

Zandi's eyes said that she didn't have time to listen to the old man now. "I have to be on time." If she got the new job there would be more money, as well as a housing subsidy. They could then move into a house made of bricks and rent out the zinc one. "If I get the job you will further your education, even if we eat once a day."

And then her eyes pleaded: You *have* to tell Grandpa about this. I cannot do it, not today. And we can no longer hide it from him.

David's eyes answered: Now you're passing this thing onto me. All you're thinking about is this new job. Who says you're going to get it anyway? Good things don't happen to us. Those who wait for the moon wait for the dark. Why should I stay behind here every day, just because I don't have a job, and have to put up with an old man's revenge? And his stories which are not true? *Abantu abadala ngama xoki* – the old people are liars. Koko Sedubedube is not the cause of all our misery, it is too easy to believe that he is.

But David knew that his eyes were speaking in vain. Zandi would leave, as she did every morning. And then he would have to tell Grandpa the secret.

Zandi took her handbag. "Tell him," she whispered softly before leaving. David decided not to answer. He was scared of starting an argument and making her difficult day harder still.

The soapy water in the tin bath felt pleasantly warm on his cold hands and arms. As he helped with the washing, he thought about the events of seventy years ago in the land of his grandfather's father. He knew the story so well, so very well. He'd heard it hundreds of times.

When Koko Sedubedube's two children got sick, the wife of Eliyasi, David's great-grandfather, was accused of causing their illness. Her hut was burned down. In the dark, Eliyasi saw a figure that looked like Koko hurrying away. The case was taken to court and the magistrate summoned Eliyasi to appear. Eliyasi had trouble in finding decent shop clothes for his appearance in court. The jacket was too tight and the shoes pinched.

And then there was the dismay Eliyasi felt at seeing all those people in that huge courtroom. The clothes that the judge's counsellors wore hung from their backs like the *mtika* that the Gcalekas used to wear in the old days. The judge himself left Eliyasi speechless. His hair was so strange and white that it made him look like a spirit.

Eliyasi was told to speak the truth. When he was asked to raise his right hand, he did so with pride. Everyone could see that the first joint of his pinkie was off. The mark of a true Gcaleka.

Then a huge man to the left of Eliyasi rose up like a cobra in long grass – that is how Grandpa always described it as if he had been there himself. The cobra told Koko's side of the story. He spoke for a long time and everything he said was a lie.

But, despite this, Eliyasi kept saying *"ewe"* while the cobra spoke. Because no Gcaleka can keep on talking if he thinks you're not listening to him. If you don't say anything he will stop speaking and say that he will not speak to a deaf and dumb person. That is why Eliyasi kept saying *"ewe"* while he waited for his chance to tell the right story.

But then the cobra stopped talking, stared at Eliyasi and spoke softly with the judge. The judge's face grew red and he spoke harshly. The interpreter then told Eliyasi why the judge was so angry. The judge did not believe Eliyasi because he was telling the court two stories. He had told the magistrate one story before this and now he kept saying *"ewe"* to another story. Koko's story. He had lied under oath and that was why he had lost the case and Koko had won. He was lucky that he was not being sent to jail.

Outside the courtroom Koko pushed his chest out proudly and praised himself with a praise song, walking behind Eliyasi all the way to the river. There Koko's nose was smashed by Eliyasi's fist. And because Eliyasi knew that Koko would take him to court again, he took to his heels with his wives and children. He and his sons came here to the city and worked with pickaxes.

David knew all too well how Grandpa's stories ended. Nothing would ever come right again until Koko Sedubedube's descendants had been punished. Grandpa did not understand that every person had his own Sedubedube whom he blamed for every misfortune in his life. Suddenly David decided to tell Grandpa that very moment, come what may. He simply could not remain silent any longer. He would never know peace until he was freed of this legacy of revenge. This problem that was eating away at his insides, might be the reason why he had not yet been able to find a job. It must surely be showing on his face all the time, he thought.

"Grandpa," he said, "there is something I have to tell you."

Grandpa did not look up. His lips moved. Was he listening at all?

"Grandpa, I know where Koko Sedubedube's people are. The man who lives with your daughter, Peace, is Koko's grandson. Zandi heard it from someone who was at the shebeen."

The old man sat upright with a jolt as if a snake had bitten him. His eyes stood still in his head. David's heart beat like a drum. What if Grandpa dropped dead? And if he didn't, what would his next words be? That David should go and kill the man who lived under the same roof as his mother? If only Zandi were there. She had a way with Grandpa. With her soft voice and fast words she would probably have been able to talk him into laying down the spear.

David fled from the house to fetch more water from the tap. Before he came back in, he heard a soft cackling laugh coming from Grandpa. David's hands tightened around the pot. Had Grandpa lost his senses? There was surely nothing to laugh about.

Then he looked into Grandpa's eyes and saw no sign of a war there.

"It is good then," Grandpa said. "Nobody could think of a better punishment for the descendants of Sedubedube than to land up in the hands of my daughter Peace."

"*Ewe*," Grandma agreed as she rubbed the washing in the soapy water with her hard bare hands.

David could scarcely believe what his eyes were seeing and his ears were hearing. I am free, he thought, free of Grandpa's revenge. Free to carry on with my own life. His legs felt lame as he wandered outside.

It was still icy cold. But he knew that when the frost lay as it did that morning, it would turn into a beautiful day.

It seemed as if the sun was setting right behind the tin shack. And it did turn out to be a good day after all. All day the sun heated the shack to the warmth of a hatched egg. And it was not a snake that was hatched, but peace. Grandpa seemed deep in thought, but contented and peaceful. Grandma's washing came out sparkling clean. David listened to the iron making its thump-thump sound inside.

He sat on his haunches in the last patch of sunlight, waiting for Zandi to return. And he thought, if the biggest problem in their lives could be so easily solved then why could other troubles not also be overcome? Why could more good things not happen to them? Why could Zandi not get that new job? She had worked for it. She always said, "All the help you need can be found in your own two hands." And "*Ewe*," Grandpa always agreed with her, adding, "Only the ox that is willing to stand up is helped to its feet."

Why couldn't he too, through his own effort, make a breakthrough?

While he waited for Zandi he composed a praise song for the two old people.

> *Abantu abadala ngama xoki*! Old people are liars!
> But only sometimes and out of love
> May God forgive those whose flesh is withered like winter grass
> Those who stumble like crippled children in the race
> Which they once ran with such swift feet
> Because I too will one day be where they are now
> But now I am still young and want to live
> I want to be a human being among other human beings
> *Ubuntu*

Then he saw Zandi coming from far away down the road. Her head bobbed faster than her pumping feet and she swung her bag high in the air as she ran.   *C. v. W.*

Engela van Rooyen was born in Kakamas on the Orange River in 1939. After matric, she went on to the University of Stellenbosch. Her writing career of 38 years includes writing for magazines and radio, and fiction. Twenty out of the more than one hundred publications are for children or teenagers. Some of the children's books have also appeared in English, among others *Die ding – The thing*, and *Jan Môre en die hamer – Johnny Later and his hammer*. Her best-known books for teenagers are probably *Kaboep en Koer*, *Gesie van Sonsig* and *Die duiwe van Botala*. Her novels for adults include *Vollermaan* and *In die oog van die web*, and most recently *Met 'n eie siekspens*. She had also taught and worked as fiction editor for *Rooi Rose* magazine. She lives in Pretoria.

Zulfah Otto-Sallies

A better life for you, Mums

It was early morning when Solly woke up. His heart was heavy. He felt frustrated and sick with worry. I must get moving, the damn trains are always so full in the morning, he thought. "Bloody Manenberg line's always a hell of a rush," he mumbled irritably to himself.

Solly glanced into his mother's room. Yakoob, his youngest brother, lay curled up next to her. *Wat gat o's maak*, Mums? he thought. For three years I've been looking for a decent job. Matric with exemption and for what? To get up every damn morning so early for another day's hard labour? "Boy", that's what they call me. A common labourer, that's what I am, Mums.

He picked up the blanket that had slipped off and carefully covered his mother and little brother. I'm sick and tired of this place, Mums; *siek en sat van sukkel*; there's not a single calamity that hasn't hit us yet, the voices rang in his head.

Last night when his mother came home, she collapsed on the chair, staring straight ahead. "The factory's closing down, Solly," was all she said. During the night Solly heard her crying. And my father is such a waste of time, Solly thought, good for nothing, that's what he is. Haven't seen him since I was twelve. With a heavy heart Solly closed the front door behind him. *Ek moet anner werk kry*; the four of us will never survive on R150 a week.

On the train he listened to the conversations. It was all about a strike at the biggest bakery in town. The men threatened with violence if other people were appointed in their jobs.

I only ask for money to put food on our table; these guys still have time to strike, the voices in his head argued again. What about you, Solly? At school you were the front runner during the political riots. Shouted for justice and democracy, and now, Solly? Mums worked herself silly to get you through matric. You were a different guy then, even went to prison for attending illegal political meetings. The state of emergency was another story. Young and old suffered during the riots for equal rights. But now the only thing that matters, is food in the house.

At school he had dreamt of going to university, of becoming rich and buying a big house for Mums. That's something of the past now. When the train stopped at Cape Town station, Solly pushed his way impatiently through the passengers to get out. Yes, he could forget about his dreams!

At the work site Solly thrust the spade wildly into the wet cement. He heard the foreman screaming, "Boy, there's too little cement here at the top!"

"Boy *se moer*," Solly mumbled.

The Xhosa man working next to him, burst out laughing and mumbled something in Xhosa to him.

During the tea break Solly sat alone and ate his sandwich with its thin spread of left-over bobotie. The Xhosa man walked over. He sat down next to Solly and offered him a mug of black coffee.

He began speaking to Solly in broken English. "I'm Sabu," he said. Sabu was full of jokes and it was not long before he and Solly became engrossed in conversation. They even poked fun at the foreman's bald head.

After work Solly and Sabu walked to the station, still deep in conversation. At the station Sabu saw one of his friends and called him over. They started talking, and Solly waited on one side. What were they talking about? He couldn't understand a word of Xhosa. Sabu suddenly called out excitedly to Solly to come over. His friend had a better job for Solly and himself, he said. They could make a lot of money. Solly felt his heart racing with excitement. Five thousand rands! Sabu said. Five thousand – if he could sell a thousand mandrax in Manenburg! Yet Solly's first reaction was: *Maak lat jy wegkom*, get away from here.

Selling mandrax! He knew what that would mean. Mums would kill him, but then again, five thousand rands! He would be able to buy so many things for Mums, the voices argued.

Solly could feel sweat forming on his forehead. Sabu and his friend were waiting. Come on Solly, urged Sabu's friend. Sabu took Solly by the arm and they walked with Sabu's friend to a taxi.

The man in the taxi passed Sabu a box stacked with packets of cigarettes. Confused, Solly walked back to the station with Sabu. Sabu explained that the mandrax was in the bottom packets. He passed the packets to Solly, who nervously slipped them into his rucksack.

That night, Solly was very quiet at the table, his mind on other things. He would contact China, he decided. China would help him sell the mandrax. China had left school in standard seven, but he had become one of Manenberg's most notorious gang leaders.

By the end of the following week, Solly handed twenty thousand rands over to the taxi owner. One thousand of Solly's five thousand rands went to China but four thousand was in his own pocket. Solly's excitement was mingled with fear. One thing bothered him. How would he explain the money to his mother? On the way home, he passed a leather shop. On the spur of the moment, he decided to buy a wallet. I'll tell Mums I picked it up, he said to himself.

That night when Solly came home, his arms were numb from carrying all the groceries. Now Mums can make us a nice pot of breyani, he thought. I've even bought her saffron! His mother was ecstatically happy, she threw her arms in the air and thanked God for this gift of mercy. "But Suleiman," she said, suddenly serious, "where does this come from?"

"Picked it up, Mums. There was no name or number on the wallet, Mums. *Dis sieke ma' onse geluk.*" His mother did not comment any further. All she did, was help him unpack.

Solly's life changed drastically. He spent most of his days organising together with China, who was called "The Don" by his friends.

More and more new things found their way into Solly's home. Yusuf and Jakoob each got a bicycle. The children from next door fought with each other for a ride on the new bicycles. Solly started going out more and more often in the evenings. He kissed Mums, just said, "*Ek ga' bietjie yt,*" and returned in the early morning hours.

By the time Solly's mother realised something was wrong, he already had his own group of dealers. Strangely enough, he could not lie to her when, one day, she questioned him directly about the source of his money.

She was hysterical and wanted to throw him out of the house. For the first time Solly screamed back at her. "I completed matric, and for what? There's still no food on our table. Just think, Mums, what happened to you. All those years Mums worked for that Jew and what did you get in return? A note on the door: *Factory closed down.*

Please collect pay at office on Friday. I'd rather go to prison, than to see you suffer again, Mums. For three long years I tried to find a decent job. This whole country's in a mess. There's no work for us. *Ek smokkel, ja, Mams, vi' kos innie hys*. And if I get punished, it's my problem. If I go to jail, at least I'll know Mums has enough money to buy bread."

His mother burst out crying. "*Is djy kla' gepraat?* I didn't raise you for this. Even if I had only bread in my house I was always grateful. All these fancy things in the house are unnecessary. *Djy is die oudste, Suleiman, en ek heddit nie van jou verwag nie.* To go to jail for something as stupid as this. Do you think it's fun 'n games in there, with murderers an'd all those kind of skollies?" She sank down helplessly on the chair and covered her face with her hands. Solly sat down in front of her.

"I'm sick and tired of poverty, Mums, *ek kan dit nie mee' vattie*. It's a way of getting rich quick. You'll be able to buy anything your heart desires, Mums."

His mother pushed him away.

"*Kanalla*, Mums, don't push me away."

"Quick rich schemes, you say, where will that get you? In the morgue, I say. *Daa' eindig allie ouens wat met drugs sukkel.* I don't need worries like that. You either stop this nonsense or you get out of my house."

Solly grabbed his jacket and stormed out of the house. He knew his mother wouldn't sleep, she'd wait to hear him come in through the front door. But nevertheless, he was on his way.

The following morning Solly and his mother did not speak to each other at all. Solly knew she was dying to speak to him, but he rather looked away. "Your clean pants are in the room," – that was the only thing she said. "*Tramma kassie*, Mums," – and that was all.

The signs of Solly's business became visible all over the house. Yusuf and Yakoob started boasting about their big brother Solly. Their school shoes were brand-new, and the sweat-suits they wore for Labarang were extra smart. There was new furniture in the house and a telephone. Solly's mother looked at all these things with dazed eyes. When the neighbours became nosy, she kept to herself.

One winter evening Solly overheard his mother saying to Yusuf, "I wish winter could last right through this year, that way Solly will have to stay indoors because of the rain. These late nights are no good." Solly wanted to comfort her, but it felt as if a wall had sprung up between them.

It was not long before Solly and China came home in a white Mercedes. Not a new one, but posh enough. China drove in circles in front of the house. Solly's mother angrily closed the windows when she saw the neighbourhood children rushing towards the car. Every night afterwards China came to pick Solly up at the house. "My chauffeur," laughed Solly.

One night, Solly said to his mother, "Mums, let's move away from this god-forsaken Manenberg, *ek kan die plek nie mee' vattie.*"

"I don't want a cent of your mandrax money!" she screamed and slammed shut the door to the bedroom.

All I wanted was to see you happy, Mums, Solly thought as he pulled the front door closed behind him. He had heard China hoot outside. Three times, that was the sign. Maybe I'll stop one day, Solly promised himself, but first I must make enough money.

That same night there was banging on the front door of Solly's mother's house. Confused, she got out of bed, her heart beating in her throat. She opened the door. "Ja?" she asked in an anxious voice.

Then she saw Solly with two policemen. They pushed him into the house and shut the front door. They had caught Solly with two million rands worth of drugs, they said.

Solly didn't say a word. He kept staring at the floor. "Ya Allah, Suleiman, Ya Allah," were the only words his mother could utter. Her whole world had fallen apart. She wept as the policemen searched the house. They found nothing.

That whole night she sat up, as if in a trance. Yusuf and Yakoob wanted to know what was going on. "Go to bed, I'll talk to you later," was all she said.

The following morning she told Yusuf to look after his little brother and took a taxi to the police station. She was allowed to see Solly for a few minutes only. With trembling hands she held him by the shoulders and hugged him. There she forgave Solly for the first time – but only in her heart. A week later a letter arrived for her.

Dearest Mums

To say I'm sorry will be dishonest. I make no excuses for my lifestyle. I tried hard to get a decent job. You know how I tried, Mums. R150 was barely enough for rent, electricity and water.

What about food? In the beginning, being a merchant bothered me a lot. I wanted to stop real bad, but then I saw for the first time how happy Yusuf and Yakoob were. Nobody teased them any more, no more broken shoes and second-hand clothes.

But with you, Mums, it was a different story. You touched me deeply. You chipped a piece out of my soul every day. You never used the stuff I bought, you walked around with the same hand-made clothes day after day. As if my presents were dirty. Mums, you never even ate the nice foods I bought. And above all, Mums, you were the one I wanted to see happy. No matter how hard I tried, I could never bribe you, fact is, Mums, nobody can bribe you. *Kanalla*, Mums, I beg you to forgive me. Nobody wanted to give me a chance, so I chose the easy way out.

It is very cold inside this place and it makes me sad, Mums, that I cannot hear your nagging any more. How well I remember the prayer you said when I passed matric. "Oh Allah, lead my children onto the straight path, protect them from evil. Grant Yusuf and Yakoob the same respect towards me as Suleiman." These words ring in my ears every day, Mums.

I still have the highest respect for you, Mums, but after a while I did not know how to stop. One thing is for sure, Yusuf and Yakoob must never walk this path. Mums, you must tell them everything.

Kanalla, do not visit me here, Mums. You are too decent for this place. A letter now and then will make me happy. I end my letter with all my love and highest respect. Once again I beg your forgiveness, Mums. *Kanalla*, Mums, I ask *tamaaf* for every atom of wrong I ever did to you.

Your lost son Solly

In the end, she did not know how many times she had read the letter. The ringing of the telephone brought her to her senses. The voice sounded strange to her, almost as if she could not hear properly. The words seemed to be hanging in the air. Then – slowly, almost like an echo – the words started to make sense. "Mrs Abrahams . . . your son was found dead in his cell this morning . . . looks like a fight broke out in his cell . . . a stab wound . . ."

The telephone slipped from her hands. "I forgive you, Solly, I grant you *maaf*, my child, Suleiman my son, Ya Allah . . . my son."

Born in Port Elizabeth, Zulfah Otto-Sallies spent her childhood in the Bo-Kaap (sometimes referred to as the Malay Quarter) where she still resides today. Since the age of thirteen she has been writing combined chorus and solo songs for Malay choirs. She wrote and directed *Diekie vannie Bo-Kaap*, a musical play, and co-directed *A man for justice*, about Imam Haroen, a martyr of apartheid. With Eoan Group choreographer, Achmad Ockards, she wrote and directed *Rosa*, a Cape Malay dance musical, which was performed in 1994 at the C.I.O.F.F. 25th Jubilee Celebration at the Jahore Festival in Malaysia. Zulfah is currently writing and directing for TV, among others a documentary, *Muslims of the Cape*, for A & P Productions for NNTV. This short story is her début as fiction writer.

Jimmy T. Matyu

Pay-day murder

It was a Friday, uncannily warm and sticky. The weather bureau in Pretoria had, however, predicted a cool, overcast day. Strangely, the sky was blue and supernaturally clear.

The bureau had also missed mentioning the unnatural phenomenon of a full round moon, dancing solo in a pale African sky on a very late afternoon with a brief drizzle, known to the Nguni people as *isicoto*. Such rain falling in softness from a cloudless sky is always regarded as an ill omen by them.

The milky whiteness of the moon was marred only by a red dot which seemed to hang loosely on it, like blood oozing from a wound – something else the weather bureau had missed in its forecast.

Litha Felemntwini was struggling to put on his tattered trousers in the backyard shack rented by his mother in the run-down settlement outside Port Elizabeth, nicknamed Soweto by the Sea. As he peered out of the broken windowpane, he noticed these signs. "Shit," he swore as he caught a whiff of the stench coming from the garbage which had collected behind the shack that had been his home for the full eighteen years of his life. He looked older though, with a frightening scar running across his left cheek.

He jerked his pullover over his head. It had been bright red when he got it from his ageing washerwoman mother, who in turn had got it, second-hand, as a gift from her "missus" in Algoa Park.

Litha Felemntwini had never known the luxury of underpants, and he had devised his own by cutting the legs off a pair of long pants and wearing these under his trousers. He sat down on a rickety chair to put on his socks and shoes, all of which were badly in need of repair.

Then Felemntwini stepped out of the shack and, taking slow strides, walked towards the bus terminus. It was a hive of activity as hawkers sold everything from pieces of tree bark for muti, to fruit, braaied meat, cooked "smiley" (goat jaw) and offal, displayed on bare wooden tables, with the flies getting a first taste before the prospective buyers.

Felemntwini did not feel hungry. He went up to the front of the mini-bus queue. No one dared to question him. He was known to be a bully, in and out of St Albans Prison. To many he'd boasted that he was a "cook" at the prison.

He stepped into one of the kwelas going to the city, paid, and then moved to the back seat. He sat next to a window. He took out a zoll from his pocket, placed it between his lips, lit a match and drew on it deeply. No one protested at the offensive smell of dagga. People looked the other way and continued sharing the latest gossip from the townships.

Felemntwini was a man of few words and unsociable. When he smiled, people could never make out whether it was a smile or a snarl.

As he joined the brisk movement on the city pavements, he was quickly absorbed into the throng of workers who, some struggling with bags of groceries after a day's sweat, made their way to the city's bus terminus known as "Down Station". Others were jumping from buses and pushing to get to the shops before closing time. It was like a madhouse, but everyone looked happy, full of life, overflowing with all-embracing friendliness as they greeted each other.

Felemntwini was not going anywhere in particular. He had come to town to execute his belief of sharing with others what they earned on pay-day. He hated the thought of being called *umkhuthuzi* – robber. He took his trade seriously, and anyone who dared to differ became instant history.

He loitered for a few minutes next to OK Bazaars and acknowledged a few greetings with obvious indifference before moving across to sit on a rail next to an auto-teller. He watched the withdrawals with the cool interest of an experienced cashier. However, sinister thoughts rioted in his mind, and after a while, he ambled into an alley. Moments later he re-emerged, looking happy and satisfied with life as he stuffed some bank notes down his trouser pocket and threw away what looked like a wallet.

Nobody will ever know what happened in that alley that day.

When people are in a hurry to get home, Felemntwini thought as he lingered at the terminus, buses always seem to take their own hell of a time. He quietly watched as kwela-kwela taxis drove up with crude young conductors leaning out of their doors, invitingly shouting "Sowubatele!" to lure clients from the nearby parking lot.

Friday, as usual, was pay-day for millions of weekly-paid black workers, and the start of the weekend. It meant good meals for many who usually miss out on meat during the week and it meant parties and braais for those who love life to be enjoyed to its fullest.

Friday always brought a strange mixture of happiness and sadness, fear and frequently death. In his peculiar mind, closed to many, even to his mother, who had learned not to ask where he'd been or what he'd done during the day, Felemntwini knew these simple truths. From where he stood after walking a short distance from the terminus, he watched a crowd of people forming outside the gates of a city factory. Another common sight on Fridays. They were mostly women, old and young, waiting patiently and keeping a keen eye out for the men coming through the gates.

The most conspicuous among the women were the small-time shebeen queens clutching their tattered little entry books with lists of those who'd drunk on the tick during the week. Felemntwini's eye also caught sight of the buxom mamas who sold fatcakes and other types of food on tick and who, by noon on this Friday, were lying in wait for their debtors to pay up.

But there were among the waiting crowd also merciless *skoppers* who owned big shiny cars, with bodyguards armed with sjamboks or kerries. Felemntwini knew what ruthless people these *skoppers* were – sharks who lend out money to others on high weekly interest – because he'd once been one of their bodyguards.

He also noticed a few odd-looking people on the fringe of the crowd: women from the rural homelands who had arrived in the city the day before to collect maintenance money from their erratic husbands who shared their compound rooms with their city live-in *amadikazi*. And there were two young girls, both "pushing prams" in the lingo of the townships, who had come to harass money from the fathers-to-be to buy layettes for their unborn illegitimate babies.

Having been taught a few tricks by his former *skopper*-boss, Felemntwini knew some debtors would try to trick their creditors by sneaking through back doors or jumping over fences. He also knew they would come back to work on Monday nursing bruised bodies, swollen faces or black eyes, having been followed to their homes and given a "panel beating".

Felemntwini walked close to the crowd and was rudely brought back from his thoughts by a booming voice. "One l-i-n-e!" shouted a burly *skopper* whose two bodyguards looked equally fearsome and tough. This command was met by a sudden rush of feet trying to form a line, labourers fiddling with their pay packets or rummaging in their pockets. They all owed him money and they knew he was quick-tempered and enjoyed brutality.

"*Nika, nika*, and do not tell me stories of your mother being dead or else I'll shit on you," he said as he cut the air with his sjambok.

They paid, including the outrageous interest, without complaint – and with a smile – but under their breath they cursed him and his *izinyanya*. Normally everybody is happy on Friday – even those unfortunate enough to return home with only a half-full pay envelope.

Felemntwini had often heard commuters discuss the happenings of Friday nights as they travelled to work by bus on Mondays. They talked about women screaming in distress in the middle of the night. He knew that youths who believed in *ekuzithatheleni* were behind those screams. Some had been caught in the act and clobbered almost to death, maimed for life, or had escaped by feigning death. However, Two-boy Salaza of the Red Location was unfortunate. The angry mob that cornered him while in the act, disposed of him in little time, letting his dirty soul escape from his body. He died in shame and disgrace. Still, a large crowd attended his funeral out of curiosity, because township gossip-mongers like controversial funerals. They want to know whether the speakers are going to shower praises on the dead or whether the priest is going to say, like they usually do, the deceased had reached the end of the line – *ufikile ekupheleni komda* – or has gone to rest in Heaven.

When Felemntwini walked back to the bus terminus, he had a strange smile on his face. He looked cheeky. The various queues at the bus terminus were growing longer and longer. People were going home to Daku, Seyisi, New Brighton, Zwide, Kwamagxaki, Motherwell and Kwadwesi. The air was tense with impatience and anger. A low moan seemed to come from the crowd. Abuses about the "poor service" were hurled about with delight – dirty, unprintable swear-words. People jumping the queue were shouted at and threats of "I'll get you" floated in the muggy air.

The smell of diesel was nauseating and the rumble of buses pulling in as others moved out was deafening. This racket was aggravated by the noise coming from the commuters, impatiently jostling to board.

"Voetsek!" A devilish-looking youngster in a faded red pullover pushed his way to the front of the queue. The shoving crowd jolted to a brief halt. The word seemed to have struck the crowd between the eyes. Having secured himself the front place, the young man added,

"I don't give a shit. You can all go to hell, *zinjandini*," and scornfully eyed those immediately behind him.

It was Felemntwini. A dagga-zoll dangled between his lips as he sneered like a character in a cowboy movie. The people inched back. They were frightened. They knew he was a tsotsi and that he lived his life in the belief that survival is only for the fittest.

Then a sudden sigh filled the air. It gushed out like water breaking through a dam wall. There was no warning and it took everybody by surprise. Seconds after his show of bravado, seconds after he'd dared everybody, Felemntwini lay on the ground, helpless, no blood showing. Silent as the grave.

He was, in fact, dead.

Nobody had seen how it happened. It was uncanny and brief. Shocked, those who had been standing close to him, stepped back as if obeying a single command. People eyed one another with suspicion and fear and started exonerating themselves, saying, "Asindim," and the women asking, "Thixo ngubani lo ukhohlakele ngoluhlobo?"

There were no answers or claims of responsibility.

"Call an ambulance," a voice shouted. No one moved.

It was not surprising. It is customary in black townships not to get involved in something which would mean dealing with the police and inviting endless visits from the law.

Frightened passengers carrying food parcels, women holding their dresses up – and young children – jumped over the body as they boarded the stationary, revving bus. Seconds before, they had shown the same fear when Felemntwini abused them. Strange that they now feared him in death. "Can't someone pull the body aside? It is not our tradition to step over a dead person," an elderly man said. But his pleas fell on deaf ears. The bus pulled away.

A small crowd, growing bigger every second, soon gathered around the body, but no one dared touch it or close its eyes.

"Don't close those eyes because the police will want to take a picture of the murderer from them," a tiny man said from the back of the crowd. Necks strained back to look at the speaker. Most commuters knew of the long-standing belief among the Nguni that a picture of the killer, if he was alone with his prey at the moment of the crime, can afterwards be seen in the dead person's eyes.

All this time no one among the crowd dared to ask where the killer had vanished to. Minutes later a police van drove in under the highway where the bus terminus is situated. The crowd moved away in order to allow an arrogant-looking policeman to pass as he pushed his way through and kept on shouting, "Kom aan, beweeg, beweeg!" – reassuringly touching the firearm in the holster on his hip.

"Banjalo ke," said a voice from the crowd. This was greeted by laughter.

"Wat sê jy daar?"

But no one responded.

More questions came from the thick-set policeman. "Wie het dit gedoen? Ek meen, wie't hom gesteek?"

There was silence.

This made the cop angry. Looking around as if he'd lost something, he again asked, "Het julle nie monde nie?"

Silence again. This time disturbed only by a crackling voice on the cop's two-way radio. This soon died away. As if poking fun at the crowd or running out of patience, he suddenly boomed, "Okay. Sal die persoon wat vir die stekery verantwoordelik is, nou asseblief vorentoe kom?"

Feet shuffled as people started to move to other bus stops underneath the freeway arch. "Uyaphambana ngoku," someone said and there was some giggling. Funny, even at a time of death people still crack jokes. But who can say this voice was not angry, angry at the killing of one brother by another?

A bus pulled up, but two other policemen directed the driver to the other side of the terminus. As it moved off, some commuters ran after it. But not before the policeman shouted, "Is hier enige ooggetuies?"

There was another sudden hush. Feet stopped running. Then suddenly one shouted, "Tyhini, nithenina. Niyaligezisa elibhulu."

There was a quick shuffle of feet as the mob once again made for the bus, and a tight knot formed as they fought to get on.

The dead body still lay there, as if begging for help. The commuters who had already seen more deaths than one should in a life time, did not seem to notice or care. The bravado which used to be written all over Felemntwini's scarred face had been wiped away by death. But a sinister grin still played about his mouth, expressing all the anger, bitterness and pain of his life. Some non-believers in the Word – *Ilizwi* – started asking in a mocking fashion whether the young man would be among those who would rise on Doomsday, and on what side of the River Jordan he would be standing.

That evening, as buses drove into the township, the talk centred around the young man who had died so mysteriously. The older folks cursed to no end the children of today. The more politicised commuters blamed apartheid and its violence. And the Bible-thumpers prayed for Jesus Christ to help the world fear God.

There were many speculations. The killer must have used an *intshuntsha* – a sharpened bicycle spoke – a weapon in fashion during the forties before every other person had a gun, someone said. The din in the bus was like in a shebeen, everyone wanting to be heard over others and shouting that it was strange nobody knew who the killer was, and that even those who had suspicions had feared to come forward.

Anyone who stepped from the bus and who cared to look up would have noticed that the moon was still dancing there. But the red dot had disappeared.

In the next day's morning newspaper there was a small paragraph about the death at a bus stop of an unidentified black youth. In bland, official language it stated that no arrests had yet been made.

The killer was still on the loose, said the newspaper. Roaming the streets of the Friendly City.

Born in New Brighton, James Tyhilekile Matyu began writing at Cowan Secondary School, contributing stories and poems to the school magazine. In 1957, while still at school, he freelanced for the *Golden City Post* and *Drum*. In 1960 he opened a Port Elizabeth bureau of *Imvo Zabantsundu*. Two years later he was transferred to its head office in King William's Town, but was fired in 1964 for being a "communist", shortly after the Xhosa weekly lost its independence. He was re-employed by *Golden City Post/Drum*, to reopen its bureau in PE. He worked for *The World* from 1974 till its banning in 1977. Jimmy was the first black journalist to win the King Korn Trophy for Media, in 1992. On the one hand harassed by security police, he has, on the other hand, received wide recognition for his contributions to society and to boxing. He is currently employed as a senior journalist by *The Evening Post* in PE.

B.M.C. Kayira

The man next door

We all knew Rey as a man without a woman.

Yet, every evening there was this woman's voice coming from his room.

Now, if the voice had been just a woman's voice, the story would have been left right there, maybe. But the voice was that of a young woman weeping – not loud enough to be irritating, but plaintive enough to make one feel restless. Particularly so if, like us, you happened to be living next door.

It must have gone on for something like three weeks before we took it upon ourselves to get to the bottom of the matter.

"Oh, hello neighbours," Rey exclaimed, when he opened the door of his flat. "Come on in!" he added enthusiastically.

We went in.

We were struck immediately by the total absence of furniture in his place: no carpet, no chair, no bed – nothing, except for the built-in wardrobe.

"I hope you don't mind the emptiness of my place," Rey remarked. "I sit on the floor, and I suppose you don't dislike the floor, either?"

"Not really, except, we are in a hurry," we explained.

"In a hurry! I really wonder why anyone would like to hurry through life. It's quite short as it is, don't you reckon?" he mused, sitting in the centre of the room, flat on the floor.

"We came in connection with the noise, you know," we began.

"Noise? What noise?"

"The weeping. Someone was weeping in here just before we knocked. And it's been going on for weeks now, you know . . ."

Rey looked at us for several long moments, appearing as surprised as he probably would have been had we just told him he was an alien. "Someone weeping in here?" he finally managed to say.

"Of course," we insisted. "And a woman, at that."

Rey exploded into laughter, and laughed so much that he started coughing. "A . . . a . . . woman in . . . in Rey's room! What . . .

93

what's the world coming to?" he gasped. Then, noticing the look of seriousness on our faces, he mustered his composure, and said, "Well, I see that you mean what you say. Look around then, gents, and see if there is any woman in here."

We just stood there, looking at each other uncertainly.

There was only the bathroom to look around in, and we ended up there. Again, the emptiness of it left us with a blank look. Where was the soap? None! Where was the toothbrush? None! The towel? None! Nothing, nothing whatsoever save for the bath tub, the toilet, and the mirror.

"Do you wish to check the wardrobe, perhaps?" Rey asked, upon our return.

Was it so serious that we could go that far? Had we not gone too far already?

"Not at all," we replied, eyeing Rey in disbelief. "It does seem rather strange, though," we added.

"Strange?" he mocked. "Let me tell you, *I've* seen some strange things, guys!" And he shook with laughter again.

Perplexed, we took leave of him.

For all that, the weeping never ceased; neither on that night, nor on the nights that followed. Within a week, Rey's other neighbours called on us.

"What's going on in the other room?" they asked, as they sat down.

"We're just as concerned," we answered. And then we told them of our visit to Rey's room.

"The wardrobe, you should have checked in the wardrobe!" they said accusingly.

After a lengthy debate, marked by a generous amount of bickering, we agreed that they should pay the man a visit themselves, when night came around again and the weeping resumed.

As surely as ever, the weeping started again that evening. And, within moments, we heard a knock at Rey's door.

"Oh, hello neighbours!" exclaimed Rey, when he opened the door. "Come on in!" he added enthusiastically.

They went in.

"I hope you don't mind the emptiness of my place," he said. "I sit on the floor, and I suppose you don't dislike the floor, either?"

"It's not the floor we came for," the neighbours growled. "It's the noise . . ."

94

"Noise? What noise?"

"Look, we have the right to know what's going on in here, alright? Some woman is being abused here, and as citizens of this country, as human beings, we ought to help."

Here, Rey went down with laughter again. He laughed so much that he started coughing. "A . . . a . . . a woman for Rey! My, what's the . . . the world coming to?" he gasped.

The neighbours went straight for the wardrobe.

The emptiness of it left them with a vacant glance: no clothes, no shoes, no bedding, no hangers – nothing, save for the compartments which make up a wardrobe.

There was nobody inside.

By now, Rey was seated in the centre of the floor. Tense silence filled the room as he and the neighbours eyed one another.

"Do you wish to check the bathroom, perhaps?" Rey finally asked.

The neighbours looked at each other uncertainly. Was it so serious that they should go that far? Had they not gone too far already?

"This is weird, isn't it?" they remarked.

"Weird?" Rey repeated. "Let me tell you, *I've* seen some weird things, folks." With that, he rose to his feet, laughing heartily.

Dismayed, they took leave of him.

For all that, the weeping did not cease. Neither on that night, nor on the nights that followed.

"We've had enough of this!" Rey's other neighbours eventually told us. "We're calling the police."

So they called the police. The police knocked at Rey's door.

"We heard someone weeping in here!" roared the police. "What's going on?"

"Someone weeping in here?" wondered Rey, standing at the door.

"You heard us right," bellowed the police.

"Hey, this isn't a joke or something?" Rey ventured after a pause.

"Buddy, since when have the police been known to joke?" snarled one of the police at him. And, with that, they pushed Rey aside. One headed for the wardrobe, and two for the bathroom.

Nothing! Nobody!

The police stood looking at one another, stupefied.

"Where do you stay?" they finally asked Rey.

"Where we are now," he told them.

He was now seated in the centre of the room, flat on the floor.

Meanwhile, the police looked at one another again, shaking their heads.

"Say, what are you playing at?" they insisted.

"Playing? Well, I'm just living, if that's what you mean," Rey responded.

"Come on, the woman. Where is the woman?" the police demanded impatiently.

At that, Rey burst into that laughter of his.

"A woman . . . a woman in Rey's place! What . . . what's the world . . . coming to?" he gasped.

"We're here on business, remember that?" warned the police, closing in.

Then, noticing the look of seriousness on their faces, Rey asked, "Do you wish to check the ceiling, perhaps?"

The police looked at one another uncertainly. Was it so serious that they could go that far? Had they not bothered themselves too much already?

They left.

The weeping continued for all that: like one of those things which you know is terribly wrong, but about which you can do nothing.

Yet, on second thoughts, was this really something we couldn't do something about? Is there really anything, in the living years, one cannot do something about?

Here, we remembered our philosophy teacher's argument, way back in college. That argument could be summarised as follows: In whatever we do, or in whatever is done to us, there is always a "yes" on our part. Explicit or implied, that "yes" is always there. Even the things we might do at gunpoint imply a "yes" on our part. Otherwise, would we do these things or allow them to be done?

Who was Rey then to impose such a lot on us? Who was Rey really to subject us to such restlessness and anxiety? All over Africa, people were beginning to say "no" to the wiles of dictators. All over Africa, people were beginning to lift their heads from the muck of unqualified reverence. All over the world, in fact, people were questioning the foundations of authority, and the propriety of servitude.

Yet here we were, reduced to passivity by nothing other than a fellow tenant. Here we were, gagged into stark muteness in the face of revolting eccentricity. Here we were, with mind and soul tantalised by one we hardly even knew. For who was Rey anyway, other than

"The man next door"? All we knew about him was that he was Rey. Rey who? None of us knew. All we knew about him was that he went out at any time during the day, and came back at any time during the night. As to his means of livelihood, none of us could even guess. We knew, also, that he was never seen with a woman. And that brought us back to the question: Whose young female voice was it, weeping in his flat?

From that point, other questions sprang up, like a bushfire which, starting with a mere spark, builds itself into a conflagration, devouring everything in its way. True, Rey was free to do in his flat exactly as he pleased. True, also, the weeping of his "woman" was not loud enough to disturb sleep, or any activity of ours. But then, there was the question of anxiety. Did Rey, or anybody else for that matter, have the right to torture us with anxiety?

Neighbours from both sides, we got together again and tried to figure out things. And so it was that, before long, we found ourselves immersed in the unfathomable issue of *freedom*.

Where really did a tenant's freedom end? Where did it start, for that matter?

We were reminded of one of the famous responses of the head of the state of Manthaland, our motherland. The story has it that on one of his trips to America, he was asked by some cheeky journalist, "Mr President, what do you say to the accusation that there is no freedom of speech in your country?"

"It's an understandable accusation," replied our hero. "The fact," he went on, "is that in my country, there is total freedom. Including the freedom to prevent others from speaking!"

There!

After another bout of intense bickering, we organised ourselves into shifts to keep track of Rey's movements outside his flat. And so we trailed him everywhere – onto the bus, out of the bus, into shops, out of shops, into pubs, out of pubs, up one street, down another street, and so on and so forth.

Here is what we found out. At no point in all his movements was Rey ever seen going into a place of work, be it an office or a building site – you name it!

Restaurants – yes, these he went into. And once there, he ate as heartily as anybody possibly could. What's more, he paid for his meals. Pubs – yes, these he went into. And once there, he drank as seriously as anyone possibly could. What's more, he paid for his drinks.

But places of work? No, never. Women? No, he never went near women.

Now, what kind of fellow was this? Where did he get the money that enabled him to live in such relative comfort – at least outside his flat? And then the final question, where did the weeping woman come from?

Ah, his contacts! We could find out from his contacts, we decided.

So, after yet another bout of debating, we launched ourselves on the trail of those people whom Rey had been seen talking to.

Nothing, nothing whatsoever!

Of the people we saw him talking to, fifteen didn't even know his name, seven didn't remember ever having talked to him, five refused to answer our questions, and two promised to beat us to rags should we ever disturb their peace of mind again . . .

Rey, what a guy!

There was only one option left. The police. True, the police had already failed. But if the police had failed, so had we. In which case, let the task revert to those who, at least, are paid to do it.

And so the police were called in again. Fuming and swearing like suppressed thunder, they burst into Rey's flat with the fury of demonstrators. "We're arresting you!" they growled.

"Arresting me, gentlemen? What for?" Rey wondered, sitting in the centre of the bare room.

"For suspicious conduct!" came the reply.

So they arrested him.

At the police station, the following morning, all the inmates complained of having heard a young woman weep all night.

Born in Malawi in 1959, Ben Kayira attended the University of Malawi between 1979 and 1983, graduating with honours. For five years he taught French at his alma mater, and since 1990 has been teaching French at the Alliance Française of Soweto. His literary endeavours include writing poetry, plays, novels, short stories and jokes. In 1990 he was co-winner of the Heinemann/ Weekly Mail Literary Award, and in 1991 won short story and poetry prizes in the African Writers' Association literary competition. He has been short-listed for an MML literary award and the APAC drama contest. This is his first short story to be published.

Elsa Joubert

Studio

Sometimes of an afternoon my editor would send for me and say,
"Leave that copy for now. I want you to fetch some pictures from
Sluytenbach. The messengers are all out."

I didn't like this picture-fetching from Sluytenbach. His studio
was in an old building downtown and the lift, which had a concertina
gate, sometimes worked but usually didn't.

I didn't like the old man either – probably not really so old, fifty-
something – because once, when his wife was out, he pressed me up
against the wall.

I didn't like his wife either. She was old and plump and her legs
were too short to reach the floor from her seat behind the desk. She
usually had the pictures ready in an envelope and had me sign for
them. I didn't like her because her hair was badly coloured and she
was wrinkled and smelt of talcum powder and she dressed in a style
that was too young for her. Also because she was sometimes abrupt –
almost rude – and other times fawned on me and tried to make small
talk.

She was abrupt if the old man was in the room with us and he
looked at me for too long and she wanted to get rid of me; she was
chatty when he was busy shooting pictures in the studio next door,
with the door firmly shut. Perhaps – who could tell? – even latched
from the inside.

He took pictures of girls.

When he was in there it was almost as though she wanted to keep
me with her, as if she was afraid. I always just took the package and
left quickly.

But he was a good photographer and my editor thought the world
of his work.

Then it happened that I got caught there by the weather one afternoon. I was still standing at the desk waiting for the envelope of
pictures when it grew pitch dark outside and flashes of lightning were
soon followed by claps of thunder, quite close by. I wasn't made for

this kind of weather, and it didn't take much to persuade me to wait until it was over.

It was one of those afternoons when the studio door was emphatically shut. After the first clap of thunder the rain came bucketing down. She switched on the standing lamp, and in the soft light the office seemed quite different. For the first time I looked around me and studied the larger-than-life-size blow-ups of his photographs on the walls.

Amazing images. The one that struck me most showed a flight of stairs, just an empty flight of stairs, but it made you feel you were going up – you climbed higher and higher as you sat there on your chair.

We heard a giggle from behind the closed door.

"Maybe she's also afraid of thunder," I said – just for the sake of saying something.

"He's a great artist," she said.

But they wouldn't be aware of the lightning in there, I realised, because the blinds were always down, the black curtains drawn, and bright lights blazing from floor stands.

Once when the door was open, I looked into the studio with its blinding lights and black curtains. It looked like an operating theatre, except there was a sofa instead of a table.

"Those bright lights must make people sweat," I said.

There was another giggle behind the closed door and then silence. Suddenly the door was flung open and old Sluytenbach came into the office, asked his wife for extra globes, which she gave him, and went back again. He hadn't seen me.

But before the door closed again, I saw on the sofa in the bright light of the studio, the naked hip of a girl, lightly draped with a piece of cloth.

"Shouldn't you go and help?" I asked his wife.

She slipped down off her chair behind the desk and I noticed that two red spots of colour glowed on her cheeks.

"He always works alone. He's a great artist." She went over to a cabinet and started pulling out envelopes packed with pictures.

"I'll show you."

She ferreted about deeper in the drawers. Sitting on the floor, she pulled out old envelopes, bleached to a yellowed brown, with dog-eared corners. The envelopes lay strewn about her. She opened them up, shook the contents out, stuffed them back in again. I noticed she was concerned only with the large envelopes. She must have been looking for enlargements. Her cheeks were now flaming red, her hands trembled slightly. Her eyes gleamed. She was completely focused on what she sought.

Then she found them. She pulled the enlargements out of an envelope with damaged corners. She spread the pictures out on the floor around her. They were studies of naked female figures. Torsos, full length, half-length, taken from the front, from the back, from the side. There was a sensuous appeal in the light and shade, the textures, the skin and the proportions, which the years hadn't dimmed.

"These were taken of me," she said, after showing me one after another, "far away on a beach where we were alone. These were his first figure studies. This was the beginning."

"You're joking . . ." I began and then realised what I was saying. "I just mean . . ."

"You mean it couldn't have been me?"

I couldn't answer.

I helped her gather the pictures together and get them back into the musty old envelope; pick up the other envelopes, put them back in the drawer.

The rain had eased off, I could go . . .

The next time I went there, it was with none of the old antipathy for the woman. She must have sensed it. Before she gave me my package she said, "Come, I want to show you something."

She took me through a door I hadn't noticed before. It was half concealed behind one of the huge enlargements and we had to push through a black curtain to where the red light still glowed dimly above the chemical baths and rinsing sinks. I vaguely made out a line, almost like a washing line, stretched this way and that over the dark little room, and on the line, fixed with clothes pegs, hung the negatives. Big ones. Rows of them.

"He took these that afternoon while you were here. The afternoon of the storm. Look."

She pointed me to the sink where the developed pictures lay in the rinse water, with the black borders, the greys, the shadows and highlights fixed. All naked figure studies. The female form; the torso from the front, from the side, from the back.

I thought of the pictures she'd shown me on the floor that day.

"But they're the same," I said. "The young body, the young skin, the textures."

In the half-darkness, I couldn't see her clearly.

"These are the same pictures . . ."

But she contradicted me. Her voice was gruff. "These are the new ones," she said.

It felt to me as though we were standing in a world of ghosts, of youth relentlessly fading away. Fear rose in me, my skin went cold.

I looked at the young woman who grew ever clearer under the running water, gracefully provocative hip and shoulder, breast and knee. And as my eyes grew accustomed to the weird red gloom, her face appeared vulnerable; and as the water washed over her, it seemed to me that there before us, her limbs, her lips, her curves begged the water: keep flowing over me, keep flowing over me.

And silently in me, I heard the same plea: keep flowing over me, keep flowing over me . . .   *C. K.*

Born in Paarl, Elsa Joubert studied at the universities of Stellenbosch and Cape Town, where she obtained an M.A. in Afrikaans and Dutch literature. She started her career as a journalist and has written six travel books (with the third, *Suid van die wind*, about Madagascar, published in 1962, she made her first breakthrough as writer), six novels (the latest being *Missionaris*), two collections of short stories (*Melk* and *Dansmaat*) and one collection of children's stories. She has received numerous prestigious literary awards, and some of her books have been translated and published overseas. Her bestselling novel *Die Swerfjare van Poppie Nongena*, translated into thirteen foreign languages, has been performed locally (in English and Afrikaans) as theatre and radio drama, as well as in the United States, Britain, Canada, Australia and Europe. She has travelled widely, alone as well as in the company of her husband, writer Klaas Steytler. They live in Cape Town.

François Bloemhof

When the world began turning
the other way

Wednesday evening, and Alan stood in front of the mirror, tugging at his clothes and ruffling his hair until he had the look he wanted.

Lucille's photo was in the corner on the left hand side, next to his aftershave. He moved the bottle in front of her. It made him cross that he couldn't stay cross with her for long.

When he'd finished, he stepped outside, to his dad's car. Some of his friends were already driving, but he wasn't allowed to. It complicates things when a guy's got a girlfriend.

Or had one, because Lucille was getting tired of being a one-man woman. Either that or the guys were lying – which was more than likely, for he knew quite a few who wouldn't mind helping her get over her tiredness.

Alan's parents appeared at the front door. Then his mum slipped back inside. As usual, she'd forgotten her handbag.

His dad opened the car door for her, as he did whenever they went out. She got in and, as always, said, "Thank you."

Thank you. Have a nice day. Come again soon. Thank you. Clichéd little courtesies endlessly repeated.

They were on their way to a parent-teacher-student evening. There would be dancing as well. The new headmaster's idea to improve spirit.

Perhaps the weather would change later, but for now it was not too hot, not too cold. An inbetween sort of evening.

They arrived at the school hall and Dad parked the car. This time Mom remembered her handbag. As usual they were far too early. A teacher stepped forward and assured Mum and Dad that it was a pleasure having Alan in his class. "But he needs to pay more attention to Maths."

Alan went in search of his friend Atkinson and found him at the entrance to the hall. "I want those answers from you tomorrow," Alan reminded him.

Atkinson nodded. "Let's go outside, I need a smoke." He'd been trying since standard eight to kick the habit. "Is Lucille coming?" he asked when they'd reached the trees and he could light up.

"Why d'you want to know?" Alan asked.

"I'm only asking, okay!"

"Well, is there any reason why she shouldn't come?"

"Look, I just told you what I heard, okay? If I said nothing it would also be a crime." The glowing cigarette emphasised Atkinson's indignation.

"Ja, she's coming. Everything's okay between us, you'll see."

"Uh huh," Atkinson nodded.

The band started playing and the music drifted across the lawn to them. Even this early it was obvious that the band was trying to play music to please everyone. In the end it would satisfy no one. For some it would be too loud, and for others too boring.

Alan and Atkinson went back to the entrance. Three adult couples were swaying on the dance floor.

There was a screech of tyres. Through the open doors Alan saw a BMW gracing the parking area with its presence. Lucille emerged, quickly losing her parents and going to the bar where she ordered a glass of orange juice. She wore a green dress and matching green ribbons in her French plait.

Alan walked over to her. "I need to talk to you," he told her softly. "Outside."

"What about?" Her eyes sought out her parents who had begun to talk to a teacher. Alan wondered if she was thinking about her recent Geography marks.

"It's private," he said.

"Can't it wait?"

"No."

When they were alone outside, he asked, "Do you still want to go out with me?"

"Did I say that I didn't?"

"Well, why do you have to go to your gran's every weekend?"

"She's old."

"*You're* not."

She clicked her tongue. "What will you and I do if I don't go to my gran's? Go for walkies?"

"Why not?"

"I'm going back inside, it's cold."

He remained standing there, his arms limp against his sides. He could still smell her perfume, the same fragrance as the night when he first kissed her.

"It doesn't look to *me* like things are okay," Atkinson said, coming up behind him.

"Didn't you just see us talking?"

"Ah, get real. She talks to her mother, her father, she talks to the teachers, and these days she does a lot of talking to Peter Sharpe. That is, if it stops at talking."

Alan had heard that little story before. "You know, Atkinson, you're a nicer guy when we're having a beer. It's a pity there's nothing stronger than orange juice here."

Wally joined them. "Guess who's just arrived?"

"Emma," the other two said simultaneously.

Emma was the ugliest girl in matric. Emma jokes had been doing the rounds for a long time now.

"You should see what she's wearing. I'd describe it to you if only I could."

"Let's go and check it out, Atkinson."

"Not now. I want another smoke first."

Wally liked being the bearer of news. "And guess who else has just pitched?" he asked. Nobody wanted to guess, so he told them, "Sharpe."

"So what?" Atkinson snapped back. Only *he* was allowed to speak about Sharpe in front of Alan.

"Well, he's . . . dancing inside there. Go and see for yourself."

Alan went back into the hall. Atkinson remained behind, puffing on his cigarette. The beat of the music was faster than before.

Emma stood by the door. In her school uniform it was easy to mistake her for one of the other girls at a distance. But her dress tonight was unique. She must surely have dug it up in an attic, Alan thought. A huge silver brooch clung to her chest. She greeted him nervously, and he acknowledged her with a non-committal "Hi".

Have you heard the one about when Emma was a baby? Her mother didn't push her pram, she pulled it behind her!

Thirty or so people were on the dance floor. Alan looked for the green ribbons. Lucille's head was resting on Sharpe's flyhalf shoulder, a few centimetres below his dumb, contented face. He had one paw way down her back. Fortunately the music stopped just then. Alan walked over to her. "I have to talk to you."

"Again?" To Sharpe she said, "Peter, please excuse me a while."- The band started another tune and Alan and Lucille danced, apart.

"What's your case with Sharpe?" Alan wanted to know.

"What's *your* case? You never had all these hang-ups before."

"What's going on between the two of you?"

"Alan, you sound like someone in *Egoli*."

"Answer me."

"Or like one of those old ladies at the telephone exchange."

"Look. Do you want us to break up or what?"

She spat out a word that doesn't appear in most dictionaries, turned and walked away. He hardly noticed the people around him. He walked smack into Emma, startling her. She was forever startled by something or the other. He looked at her and then the thought entered his head. Well, why not?

"Wanna dance?" he said to her.

Emma got a fright. This time it was justified. She had just heard the unthinkable. She managed a choked "Okay" and hobbled up to him. They moved onto the dance floor. The material of her dress was coarse and he could feel her ribs underneath it. She was a poor dancer and kept stepping on his toes. He looked around for Lucille but couldn't see her anywhere.

The music stopped, but something inside him had begun to build up and he didn't know what he would do if he stopped dancing. Emma wanted to go back to the wall but he stopped her with a tight grip on her arm. They danced in silence and gradually she stepped on his toes less and less. "Have you done your homework?" she asked after a while, then realised her mistake and quickly added, "I haven't either." After a minute or so she tried again with, "It's a nice evening, isn't it?"

"Ja, sure." When he looked out the door he seemed to notice the weather for the first time.

And then the strangest thing happened. He saw that Emma had the most beautiful teeth, even and white; they reminded him of the colour of white roses. At least one quality which nature had not denied the girl.

"Let's go outside," he said.

At the bar, Atkinson was killing himself laughing. When he waved, Alan waved back. Emma thought that Atkinson was waving at her too. She responded and that made him crack up even more.

Outside in the dark, where only the crickets could hear them, they chatted. She didn't have a bad voice. She spoke in low, dark tones. She would like to be a singer one day, she confided. She hadn't told anyone else that she'd been taking singing lessons for a while now. She just had to finish matric first.

They went back in and danced some more, past Lucille and Sharpe. Lucille looked the other way.

Then it was time to go home. The headmaster told them how sorry he was that the evening had come to an end so soon.

Alan stepped aside to let Emma pass. "Okay, see you around," he said.

"Bye."

He walked towards the door, but something made him turn around and he saw her face in the one moment she forgot to keep it neutral. She got a fright when she saw his eyes on her and quickly looked past him. "I er . . . wonder where my parents are. They . . ."

"Maybe outside already." He wanted her to go. What had he done?

"Uhm, yes," she said, "I'll go and see." Her movements were hesitant, tense. He expected her to look back, but she didn't.

That look on her face. Did he ever look that way himself? Had Lucille ever noticed, and if she had, how was it possible that she didn't care?

He found his parents. His dad gave him a funny look, but what the hell, he would dance with whom he pleased. Then again, she *was* ugly. But that wasn't her fault – or his. He needn't feel he owed her something.

They drove home in silence.

His mum remembered her handbag. His dad opened the car door for her. Again Alan had the feeling that his dad was looking at him just a little too closely. His dad liked Lucille, he'd said so often enough. And she really was very pretty, no denying that.

Later, he lay in bed, awake in the dark. The door opened and his mum came into the room.

"I did say goodnight," he said.

"I know."

She came closer. Her perfume had a floral fragrance. She bent over and kissed his forehead. She hadn't done it for years. A faint glow from the passage cast some light on her face. Her features appeared almost perfect, just like they once must have looked before time, with its uncharitable hands, came to touch her.

"You must get some sleep now," she said. "It's school tomorrow."

C. v. W.

François Bloemhof was born in Paarl, spent his childhood in various small towns and studied at Stellenbosch before settling near Cape Town – the only place to live, he says. He is the author of four Afrikaans novels dealing with topics not normally pursued in Afrikaans: Gothic horrors on the platteland, Satanism in suburbia and curses that cause farms to thrive while also destroying those who live there. He is a lover of books, music, cats and chocolate. His books are *Die nag het net een oog*, which won the De Kat Prize for best first novel in 1991, *Die duiwel se tuin*, *Koue soen* and *Bloedbroer*. He has also published a large number of short stories in Afrikaans and English in South African magazines, some of them under a pseudonym.

Marguerite Poland

Mother, daughter

JUNE 13TH 1967:

The other day I found a book to write in and a box exactly the right size. It's not very big but it has a hasp and staple for a padlock and it's strong. It's an oblong camphor thing that I saw in Putneys' window in Main Street nesting inside other boxes, carved the same. It's supposed to be exotic and I thought it was because it comes from China, but Mum just says it's kitsch. Still, I have things to put in it which no one must find. To other people the things would probably seem ordinary, or silly. There are a whole lot of letters and a small packet of beach sand emptied out of my jeans' pocket and one of his Texans shedding tobacco in little wisps all over the place. I've also put in the chit for the coffee and chips from the Silver Slipper Cafeteria with the winking blue sign and the neon moon at the back of the Walmer Drive-In. We felt bad sitting there eating "slap" chips, knowing that the township children, hanging about on the other side of the fence, were peering between the Port Jacksons to catch a glimpse of the screen. To make up for it, I turned up the volume on the speaker – but the wind always howls so much, no one could have heard. Imagine *Lawrence of Arabia* without the theme tune!

Besides the Texan and the tickets, there's the carnation with a rubber band around it from last night. We went to the Sky Roof to dance. It sounds romantic but it's not. It's only four floors up in an old hotel overlooking the parking lot on the beach. Without asking, he ordered me some cocktail with a little stick and an olive. It looked very grand and sophisticated. And I suppose that's what he wanted me to be. Grand and sophisticated – *me* – with my hair all done up and aching at the roots and my sister's false eyelashes, stuck on wrong. He sat there with a sort of half-smile on his face, watching me. Perhaps he thought I'd fall off the bar stool. I nearly did. And suddenly, it seemed he'd done all this before, lots of times, long before he knew me.

I don't remember ordering food. It just arrived, sole decorated with a radish flower and piped potatoes. I can still see the carnations in the vase turned upside down in reflection in my glass. I really had to concentrate on what I was doing. But he was quite at home, even bored, like he came here every week. It was the first time I couldn't think of anything to say. He seemed so awesome and distant, sitting there across the table with his Texans. Not like before when we went to the drive-in. Not like when we walked on the beach or fished off the rocks or explored the dunes on Sundays. Not like that at all.

I have also put the poems that I wrote in the box. I thought they were okay. They're not. They're dreadful. All about African moons and stars and things. Once, he wrote a poem too. It was so good, I think he must have cribbed it. I kept remembering the last lines as we were driving home, turning up the hill away from the harbour and seeing the lights curve out beside the breakwater and far along the bay.

> From these and others have I turned
> and followed the night out . . .
> and passed the reaches of the town

We went, driving without speaking, following the night out. Past the reaches of the town. Just like the poem. There was something very final in it all.

26/06/94:
I will always remember last night. That's why I am writing about it in this book I found in Mom's cupboard. She probably won't notice that I've taken it but even if she does, I don't think she'll fuss, which is odd, because she usually fusses a lot about really trivial things. Anyway, I need to write this down and it has to be in something lasting. Not something that I'll throw away. I have to hold on to it. When I've finished, I'll put it in my box.

I have had to get a padlock for the box. I didn't want to – but if I hadn't, someone would have snooped around in it. If Mom goes in there she'll have this urge to tidy up all the stuff from his Leavers' Dance, like the dead flowers from the table-setting and the paper serviettes and the name cards and the withered-up balloon. She might even look at his letters although it's a matter of honour that she wouldn't read them. But how can I know for sure? And then she might find this. And I want to keep what I've written secret. Because it is. If anyone sees it, it won't be special anymore. If I tell about it, it will sort of disappear. If I try to explain it, my friends will want to add their own story as if it was like this for them as well. They'll make it ordinary. That is always the worst part. People who make things ordinary.

JUNE 13TH 1967:
Everyone was in bed when we got home. I tiptoed in and said to Mum, *I'm back*. She asked what the time was and I said eleven, though it was nearer twelve. Curfew's twelve and no excuses. *Ever*. I closed the door and went to the kitchen and we made coffee and we took it to the fire which was still burning in the lounge and we turned out the lights because the twelve rule applies in and out of the house and he was supposed to have gone. You can talk by the fire because it reaches only far enough to let you see each other and to shut the ordinary things away in shadows. We put cushions on the rug. We listened to the wind high up in the chimney and we could hear the dikkops, far outside, calling on the lawn. He talked. I don't know why he told me all the things he did and why I let him say them – except I knew I'd never have a chance to hear them all again. On and on, explaining. And funny, when he stopped, I felt . . . kind of powerful and tender – for pretending not to mind. And doing it so well.

He was still there when the fire went out, even after all the things he'd said.

That's when Mum came in. She sent him away. Just quietly, not shouting or anything. And when I'd said goodbye and gone to my room, I found she'd turned back the sheets and smoothed the eiderdown and kind of tucked it in. It was a funny thing to do.

26/06/94:
About last night. We went to watch Natal playing Province and then we went to Rovers. Everyone was there. Absolutely everyone. All back for the varsity vac like him, drunk and acting heavy and talking about "babes" as if I wasn't there. You'd think they didn't know me from before. You'd think I'd never watched each match they'd ever played at school last year. They really hacked me off. He did too, for acting like them. I hate his goatee anyway. I wish he'd shave it off.

To make it worse – *embarrassment* – Mom rocked up at quarter past eleven to fetch us! She wouldn't even let one of his mates drive us home! She seems to think he's still at school! Never mind the long hair! Never mind the earring! And she had *that look* when she saw him. So we drove home and no one talked. I couldn't think of anything to say. Not with him so different.

We made coffee like we always used to do and took it to the TV room. But you can't talk in a lighted space in the middle of the house with the TV on so that no one hears you. I kept feeling the draft coming down the passage and the screen kept blinking along like someone sitting there, listening. He seemed all restless so I took him to my room and closed the door. We sat on the floor with the duvet round us. And even though Dad has said that the one important rule is that you may never, ever take a guy to your room in this house, I took the chance because there was nowhere else to go where we could talk and be alone. And it was too important.

I don't know what he wants anymore.

Because what he wants and what he says are different things.

And what I want and what I say have always been the same.

Perhaps he's feeling trapped. He's pretending to himself he isn't, but I know. It's funny how it made me sort of want to rock him, quietly, as if I didn't really mind. I don't know why – but when it's dark, there's only *now* and the rest doesn't seem to matter. Not till later anyway.

Then Mom came.

I heard her first, going slowly because the lights were out. I went to her, angry – and frightened – knowing that she'd shout. She didn't. I don't know why. She just waited till he'd gone and when I came back to my room she'd picked the duvet off the floor and folded it and made it neat.

JUNE 13TH 1967:
I always knew he'd have to go. Back to where he came from, when the winter holidays had passed. He told me from the start. It's as if he'd dared to make it special just because he knew that it would have to end soon. This time and nothing more.

I wonder why he chose tonight instead of Sunday when we were fishing down at Schoenies? Perhaps he thought that an "occasion" should mark the final scene and that with others around I wouldn't cry and make a fuss. Or poke my rod in his eye. Or throw myself into the sea . . . And in the end it seemed like I was comforting him. At least, that's what he'd planned that I should think. It made him feel better.

26/06/94:
I wonder why tonight? Why not last time, at the Leavers' Dance at school? End of term. End of year. End of school. "Bye-bye, little girl." I just remember that we laughed a bit, walking with the others to the hostel bus, waiting in the parking lot. Holding hands, we made our shadows link and part – one, then two . . . two, then one. They followed on beside us on the grass. It was a silly game but at that moment nothing could have spoiled it. Not ever.

I wish we'd left it like it was.

I wish he'd stayed away.

He doesn't even look the same.

JULY 30TH 1967:
I've been waiting for a letter but it hasn't come. I suppose it never will. He said he wouldn't write. He said it should be left – perfect – as it was. Big deal. Did he think it was a story or a play with <u>The End</u> neatly underlined? I don't suppose that characters can rise from books to argue with their authors.

Perhaps I'll meet him in a street one day.

Perhaps then I'll be famous and he won't.

Perhaps it's me, not him, who'll decide on how the postscript's going to be.

17/07/94:
It's nearly three weeks and I haven't felt like writing in this book. I thought I'd fill it all – and now, there's nothing that I want to say. It's because I've just been waiting for the phone, even though I know he's not going to call.

I wish I could explain it to myself.

I wish that there was someone I could tell.

JULY 30TH 1967:
Some secrets shared make strangers out of people after all. It's such a contradiction, but it's true. Daytime always brings some great betrayal. Why is that? If I could ask, I would, but there's no one who

would really understand, who wouldn't spoil it all by trying to explain.

That's why I'm writing this.

Then I'll lock it in my box.

Perhaps one day, years from now, I'll have a reason to remember.

Born in 1950 in Johannesburg, Marguerite Poland grew up in Port Elizabeth and holds a B.A. in Xhosa and Social Anthropology (Rhodes), an Honours in African Languages (Stellenbosch) and an M.A. for a study of Zulu folktales (Natal). She has worked in the S.A. Museum in Cape Town, as welfare officer in KwaZakhele, Port Elizabeth, and at the Institute for Social Research at Natal University. Her publications include children's books (*The Mantis and the Moon, The Woodash Stars, The Bush Shrike*), novels (*Train to Doringbult, Shades*) and non-fiction. She has received the Percy Fitzpatrick Award and the Sankei Honourable Award (Japan), both for *The Mantis and the Moon*; her novels for adults have been shortlisted for the CNA Literary Award and M-Net Book Prize. She lives in Kloof and is currently working on a Ph.D. in Zulu studies.

Chris van Wyk

Relatives

When I was twenty-one I went down to the Cape to write a book. I had got it into my head that my first novel should be a family saga and that my own roots could be found in the arid dust of the Karoo, that famous semi-desert in the Cape, in a little dorp called Carnarvon.

I had first gone down to Cape Town for a week. How could one travel all the way to the Cape without a trip to the most beautiful city in the world, Table Mountain, the train ride from Simon's Town to the city meandering along the beach, the beautiful coloured girls with their lilting, singsong voices?

Then back to Hutchinson Station in the heart of the Karoo to be picked up by my grandfather's younger brother, Henkie. A bigger version of my oupa, Uncle Henkie's other difference was that he had mischief in his eyes where my oupa had brooding shadows.

Then followed an hour's drive to Carnarvon by way of long, hot, dusty, potholed roads past waving, poor people on foot or pushing bicycles, and carrying bundles of wood or things wrapped in newspaper.

Carnarvon was a place in the middle of nowhere where nothing happened. Simple breakfasts, lunches and suppers were linked together by chains of cigarettes and conversations consisting of long, trailing life histories that made the old men in their elbow patches stammer and squint into the past from behind their thick spectacles, as they dredged up anecdotes from the dry riverbeds of history.

Oh, how wonderful it was listening to those minutely detailed sagas. But after two weeks I was bored out of my wits. The novel could wait, I decided as I packed up and was driven back to Hutchinson Station. The train from Cape Town – the very same one that had brought me there two weeks before – slid into the station. I bade Uncle Henkie goodbye with a promise that I would feature him prominently and truthfully in my novel.

When the train slithered out, I turned to the passengers in the compartment with whom I was going to spend the next sixteen hours or so on the way to Johannesburg.

There were three young men, two bearded, two chubby. (If you think I can't count, remember the riddle of the two fathers and two sons who each shot a duck. Only three ducks were shot. Why? Because one was a grandfather, the other a father, and the last a son. The man in the middle was both a father and a son, got it?) All youthful and exuberant, they were drinking beer, straight from the can, and their conversation was full of the hammers and nails of their profession and punctuated with laughter and inane arguments. None of them swore and they all flashed smiles at me, accepting me into their midst with an easy friendliness.

"You been to Cape Town?" one of them enquired.

"Ja," I said, shoving my bag into the space above the door among their own bags and stuff.

"Then you must've got your quota of ten girls," he said with a wink.

Of course I knew exactly what he was talking about: in the Mother City there were at least ten girls to every boy. I gave them a supercilious nod, hoping to convey the impression that I had certainly got my fair share. The truth of it was very different. All I could truly claim was a brief encounter with Marina, a nurse from Tygerberg hospital. She had allowed me to kiss her in the back seat of her cousin's car, but my beer breath had proved too much for her and after administering a violet-flavoured Beechie, she bade me goodnight and told me to come and see her in the morning.

There were two other passengers in the compartment. They were not quite as friendly as the trio from the Cape. They sat huddled in a corner, muttering in undertones and casting sidelong glances down the green SAR leather seat at me and my new buddies. They were brothers. This was obvious from their identical features: sandy hair that had been cut so short that the hairs grew in sharp italic spikes. They both had dark, brooding eyes and thick pouting lips. They wore khaki shirts and pants.

Try to describe people you meet on a bus or train it said in the writer's manual. I slipped a blank sheet into my mental typewriter and went to town:

They sit huddled in the corner of the compartment, bent so low in their conniving that they almost stick to the green SAR leather like two unsightly stains. They are identical but for the fact that there is a two or three year difference between them. Juveniles in khaki, they look like fugitives from a boy scout patrol, runaways not prepared to abide by the rules of the Lord Baden Powell. Stripped of their badges, their epaulettes, their scarves, banished to ride forever, second class on the Trans-Karoo.

As I've said, I was only twenty-one at the time.

I turned away from them and back to the three big men who were asking me questions as if I was an old buddy. I was surprised and pleased by this unexpected attention and friendliness. One of them glanced at his watch from time to time and stared out of the window at the scrub that made up the dry, lonely landscape of the Karoo. They asked me how my journey down to the Cape had been. They all seemed genuinely interested. One of them slid a can of beer across the little panelite table. They all sat forward to listen to what I had to say. I lit a cigarette, passing the pack around to my three friends. Then I began a story which I had already tested on my uncle in Carnarvon. There, among seasoned storytellers, it had passed my "litmus" test – Listenable, Interesting, Telling, Meaningful, Unusual, Strange. I knew I had a winner:

On my way down from Johannesburg my travelling companion – no one else had been booked into our compartment – had been a Capetonian man. He travelled in a flamboyant striped yellow and white suit, every time he spoke he injected an air of drama into the compartment, and when he was quiet he seemed all the time to be sizing me up. I remember his name, Georgie Abrahams, from Elsies River.

As the train started its long journey out of Johannesburg Station, Georgie began to tell me how he had once killed a man. Where? In a compartment exactly like the one he and I were sitting in, facing each other. Why? Because, Georgie was very eager to explain, this *skelm* tried to steal some of Georgie's possessions: food, money, an expensive watch? I can't remember what it was but Georgie caught him, beat him up, sliced him from his greasy fat neck down to his "klein gatjie" – Georgie's words. He threw the remains of the dead man out of the window in the dead of night, and wiped the blood carefully from the windowpane, the green leather seat, the floor. When the conductor questioned the whereabouts of the missing man, Georgie merely shrugged and uttered a melodious "How should I know? Nobody asked me to take care of him."

But even as Georgie was relating this tale of theft and murder in all its horrific detail, I knew it was a lie, simply a more elaborate version of my mother's dire warnings to yours truly at seven, "If you eat in bed you'll grow horns", or the more convincing "Go to bed with wet hair and you'll suffer from a smelly nose for the rest of your life". Georgie was in fact warning me to stay clear of his luggage! And the story had quite an amusing ending. When we reached Cape Town Station, a toothless woman in a lopsided jersey, stretched to twice its original size (which used to be XL) welcomed the murderer home with an unceremonious slap across his face, while I looked on together with a brood of his startled children who didn't know if they should laugh with delight at their papa's homecoming, or cry for the humiliating onslaught he was being subjected to.

"Ses maande en djy skryf niks, phone niks, not a blerry word van djou!"

My companions chuckled. They couldn't decide what was better, my story or my Cape accent.

I looked at the two sulking boys in the corner. They had followed the entire story, but they refused to laugh. So what! It hadn't been for their amusement anyway.

But then my journey took an unexpected turn. An hour or two from Hutchinson my three companions got up, stamped the pins and needles out of their feet, swept the crumbs from their pants and began to gather up their luggage. They shook my hand, slapped my back and said goodbye. And at the next station they were gone. It all happened so quickly that I was a little stunned. Now it was just me and the kids in khaki. And then a strange thing happened. I suddenly knew why they were dressed in khaki. In all probability they were from a Cape Town reformatory on their way home to Johannesburg! Why had I not realised this simple fact before? The answer was elementary. I had been far too preoccupied with my new friends to pay too much attention to these two boys and there were no guardians in sight. But now that I was alone I focused my attention full square on these two, and in an instant I realised where they were from.

The two juvenile delinquents also seemed to undergo some transformation. They no longer muttered but spoke loudly, spicing their conversation with vulgarities. And, in an act of territorial imperative, they claimed more than their fair share of the confined space, stretching their stocky legs along the seats, putting their luggage everywhere, littering the floor with clothes and greasy food packets.

Then they began a conversation which froze my blood. Their brother, the leader of a gang, had been killed by a rival gang in a Johannesburg township called Coronationville. They had been given a weekend off to attend the funeral. They would bury their brother like the hero that he was, but they vowed to avenge his death before the soil on his grave hardened. They even had an argument about how this murder would be carried out, a slow cutting of the throat was the younger's plan. No, the elder brother disagreed, stab him about a hundred times, but from the ankles to the neck.

As these plans were being discussed they kept looking me straight in the eye as if challenging me to say anything in protest or disagreement. Each time I looked away, not daring to utter a word.

Meanwhile the train seemed to be riding into the sunset. A cool breeze replaced the warmth and the grim brothers felt the cold and pulled up the windows.

I began to worry. How could I spend an entire night in a pitch black compartment with two juvenile delinquents! Maybe I could go out in search of the conductor and ask to be moved to another compartment. But if I did that my two little gangsters would know instinctively what I was up to. This also meant leaving my luggage unattended. As these thoughts went through my head, I looked down from the top bunk and saw the elder brother staring at me. He knows what I'm thinking, I thought.

Darkness came and we turned on the lights. A caterer opened our door and read out the menu for supper. The two boys ordered steak, buttered bread, and potato salad. I had no appetite. The caterer left and I heard him whistling down the corridor and opening the compartment next door. My companions glared at me again. They seemed to know why I had not ordered a meal.

On my way down to the Cape, Georgie Abrahams had joked about committing murder. This time there was no such threat – towards me anyway. But for every dark kilometre to Jo'burg I felt that my home city was moving further and further away.

"You!" I looked down from the bunk. It was the elder brother who was demanding my attention.

"Ja," I answered as casually as my voice would allow.

"Are you not Aunty Ria's child – grandchild?"

"Yes!" I could not believe my ears. Aunty Ria, as they called her, was indeed my grandmother and the mother of my own mother.

"I knew it was you when I saw you," he said, not smiling but with some friendliness in his voice. His brother stared up at me with some interest.

"You're that clever boy who used to read books and write stuff, hey?"

"Yes, but who are you?"

"Me 'n him we Aunty Visa's grandchildren."

Aunty Visa was my granny's sister.

"Then we're cousins!" I said. This wasn't quite true but I was desperate to be as closely related to them as possible.

When their food arrived they insisted that I join them. And I did, for suddenly my appetite had returned.

I had forgotten all about my chance encounter with my two delinquent relatives until the other day, three years later.

I opened the newspaper and read a report about rampant gang crime in the streets of Western Township and adjacent Coronationville. The article spoke of streets running with the blood of gangsters, the death of innocents caught in the crossfire, the revenge killings, the tragic futility of it all. The writer paid particular attention to the two brothers who had been stabbed to death and who now lay dead in the same graveyard as their brother, killed three years ago.

They had never reached twenty-one.

Born in Johannesburg in 1957, Chris van Wyk lives and works in Johannesburg as a freelance editor and writer. His book of poetry, *It is Time to Go Home*, won the Olive Schreiner Award in 1980. Books for teenagers are *A Message in the Wind*, which won the Adventure Africa Award in 1981, and *Peppy and Them*. His books for younger children are *Petroleum and the Orphaned Ostrich*, *Bubblegum Bheki* and *Wanda's Friendly Watermelon*.

Melvin Whitebooi

Looking for Johnny September

Alice's Pub is a small bar in Uitenhage. When I walked into the place late one night I noticed a distinct pause in the jovial din. Even the one-man band stopped playing (I think) and I could feel the suspicious stares turning to me from every side. This sudden lull must have lasted only a few seconds. But to me it felt like an eternity.

The barman was an elderly, stern-faced man. He looked at me with annoyance when I leaned over the counter to order a beer. (The loud noise and the music left me no choice.) Probably not every day that a white man walks into your bar and orders a drink, I thought. And a white man with a Transvaal accent to boot.

I looked around. The place was full. On a bench in one corner a man lay on his back. Life's burdens had become too heavy to bear and he was sleeping his cares away. The one-man band – a young guy with greasy hair and an earring – played sentimental songs from the sixties. A small group joined in lustily in the singing.

"So what brings you here?" a young man next to me asked out of the blue. He had an open, friendly face and short-clipped hair. He took my beer and a glass from the barman and passed them on to me.

"Just passing through," I lied, foaming up my glass with beer.

He gave me a sidelong glance over the rim of his glass.

"You know something," he said eventually, making sure that I did not avoid his gaze, "you're the first whitey ever to walk into this place. Why the Alice? Why not an all-white pub?"

"Apartheid's dead," I reminded him quietly. "It's a new South Africa. We've had our elections. And now a man can go and drink where he pleases."

"True," he smiled. "But don't we all prefer to be with our own kind?"

"Not necessarily. Even though I am a Transvaler."

"I realised that," he said. "Anyway, let me not disturb you. Enjoy your drink."

As he turned to go I put my arm on his shoulder. He turned and, for a moment, looked at me scornfully. "Don't tell me you're . . ."

"No, no," I assured him. "I'm a newspaper man . . ."

He gave me a disbelieving frown.

". . . an investigative reporter for *Beeld*, in Johannesburg."

He relaxed a little with a smile that seemed to say, I'll be your pal if you'll be mine.

"A reporter." From the way he pronounced the word it was clear that newspaper people were held in high esteem in the Eastern Cape.

"I need some help."

"What about?" he said, uncertain.

"Well, you know, we're living in a new South Africa, the old one is dead and gone, that sort of thing . . ."

He gazed at me through earnest eyes, but a smile played around the corners of his mouth.

"We're planning to do a series, on, er, coloureds, brown people, if you like, who have sacrificed just as much as blacks and whites for the new South Africa. We . . . the newspaper . . . wondered if we couldn't talk to the parents, the family and friends of people who fell under the old regime?"

The smile melted from his lips.

"What's your name?" he asked after a long pause.

Suddenly my own mouth felt dry.

"Christiaan Louw."

"And they call you Tiaan?" he asked and laughed.

I didn't laugh, but I was glad he found it funny.

"And you?"

"Joubert. Frank Joubert."

I ordered more beer. At first he was hesitant about accepting his but took it in the end.

"You know," he said later, "it's the first time I've ever had a drink with a whitey, but . . . well, you're actually not bad for a whitey."

In between beers we arranged that I would pick him up at his house the next day – after lunch. It seemed that for coloured people too, Sunday lunch was a very special occasion.

I told Frank about Johnny September, a young man from Uitenhage who had been shot and killed in April 1990. I was interested in Johnny September's story, I told him.

At the mention of September a distant look of sadness filled his brown eyes. He blinked but said nothing. Then he took a long, reflective sip of beer as if to say, Is there no end to the suffering?

He knew Johnny well, he said. In fact, very well. He would take me to meet Johnny's family. After all, it was time the world was told the story of Johnny September. Then he stood up, left half a glass of beer on the table, and walked out of the bar. I half rose to go after him, but let him go. I sat down again and stared at the foam on my beer.

That entire night I did some more staring at the ceiling. My mind refused to focus on one specific thought and instead scampered in mindless directions, tiring me out and eventually leaving me to sink into a deep sleep in the early hours of the morning.

Sunday afternoon was bleak and grey with an incessant drizzle enveloping the town. I found Frank's place easily. He lived in Blikkiesdorp, so named for the number of corrugated tin structures that dominated what was virtually a squatter camp. His house was covered in a coating of lime that had started flaking off in places. The Joubert family's tiny yard boasted the only tap for several families, and a crowd of people, all clutching buckets, clustered around it. I got out of my car and immediately felt several pairs of eyes on my back, all asking the question: White man, what do you want here?

Frank opened the door before I could knock.

"Shew! I feel like yesterday's leftovers," he groaned in greeting, looking at me through bloodshot eyes. I waited for him to invite me in but instead he took my arm and led me back to my car.

We made our way to a house that was even more run-down than the Joubert home. A piece of cardboard was stuck in one of the windows in the place of a pane. A little girl, playing with her dolls in the shade of a tree, looked up at us as we passed her. Frank and I walked to the door, both silent.

The entire family sat waiting for us in the living room. They were all neatly dressed. It made me feel uneasy. Frank had obviously told them that I was coming and I suspected that they had dressed up especially for me.

Johnny's pa: You want to know about Johnny, meneer? He was a good boy, meneer. A good boy. It's not true what the policeman said about him. He was no terroris'. Not our Johnny.

Johnny's ma: He was our only son, meneer.

Johnny's grandma: And a difficult birth it was. We thought . . . we thought it was goodbye to both of them. But they pulled through.

Johnny's pa: I worked hard to give him a decent education. You see, we just did the lower standards, me and my wife. Then he went to Jo'burg.

Johnny's ma: To Sasol, that's where he went.

Johnny's pa: I know, dear. But that's also up there somewhere.

Johnny's ma: That policeman, he jus' told lies, meneer. He was no terroris', not Johnny. His friens came an' tol' us . . . All he did was go an' drink a few beers at a shebeen with his friens. He didn' even know they were ANC. An' then that policeman went an' got himself a medal on top of it for murdering my child. Shooting him dead. Two shots in the back. He was a good child, my Johnny. Always sent us money, never skipped a month.

Johnny's grandma: Also wanted to build a house for us. He use to say this one won't last long.

Johnny's ma: But we have forgiven an' forgotten, meneer. That is what the Good Book says we must do.

Johnny's pa: I went to vote, meneer. First time in my life. An' there was such peace . . . that's how Johnny would've want it to be . . . to forgive . . . not to bear grudges against anyone . . .

Later, Frank and I drove over to Johnny's girlfriend's place. We found her sitting on the stoep, knitting. Frank had been reluctant at first to introduce me to her. He refused to give any reasons. But in the end he agreed to take me. When we arrived, Frank and this woman stared silently at each other for a few seconds. There was something in their eyes which I could not explain, something private.

Johnny's girlfriend: What can I say? There will never be another Johnny. Nor do I want one again. I'm raising our child, alone. If you had known him, meneer, you would also have understood the kind of person he was. Big-hearted, a good man. Loving. (She began to sob.) Oh Lord, meneer, I miss him so! (She wiped away the tears.) But it's all over now. We look ahead of us now. Me and our little girl. I have forgiven.

Me: Can . . . *can* one forgive?

Johnny's girlfriend: Yes. Some people forgive because they believe in the Good Book. And some of us . . . some of us forgive because we can't bear the hatred any longer, because we're tired, tired to death of it. (She pressed her fists to her forehead.) But then again, take our President, Mister Mandela. He has been through so much more than any of us, and yet *he* could forgive. Completely.

It was late afternoon when I stopped the car in front of Frank's door. We had driven back in silence. Yes, he had taken me to others who also knew Johnny, but everywhere the story was the same.

He turned now to look at me, his eyes very dark. "She left me for Johnny," he said. "And then he actually had the decency to ask me to forgive him. He disarmed me totally with this. That was Johnny for you. You couldn't help but like the man."

He opened the door. I took his arm.

"Let it be," he said, "Mandela has forgiven. Johnny's parents have forgiven. It's a new country, a new beginning."

Then he looked straight at me. "How old were you in April 1990? Nineteen? Twenty?"

My head reeled. "Did you . . . did you know all along?" I asked, my hand already extended to say goodbye.

He didn't answer, and only hesitated for a moment before he took my hand. He got out, closed the door and walked towards the house without looking back.

I didn't turn the engine back on, just sat there. Is this what I came for, I wondered. Forgiveness? To be assured that Johnny's people had forgiven us for everything that we had done to them?

There were people who had been brainwashed into believing that someone like Johnny September was a terrorist, a murderer, a dangerous man.

I know that, because I was the policeman who shot dead Johnny September.

C. v. W.

Melvin Whitebooi was born in Uitenhage, grew up in Port Elizabeth, and completed his schooling at Uitenhage High. He wrote his first short story, published in *Brandwag*, in Std 7. During his term as fiction editor of *Die Burger Ekstra* he wrote fourteen serials and also developed stories of other Cape Flats writers for publication in *Die Burger Ekstra*. Since 1985 he has been subeditor at *Rapport Metro*. He has written a number of plays, including *Dit sal die blerrie dag wees!*, *Die kant, daai kant* and *Koffie en kondensmelk*, some of them performed in professional theatres and at the Grahamstown Festival. He wrote *Die reënmaker* for radio, and for television the family serial *Die Allemans* and the play *Tot jy dood is*. Melvin lives near Eersterivier in the Western Cape.

George Weideman

Glass

Dalena showed up at my stall with the two glasses after she'd visited a small dorp somewhere in the sticks. "Jossie," she said, stumbling as usual over her own enthusiasm, "you'll never guess what I've come across." She plonked the glasses – brown and chunky – down amidst my sad little brooches.

Then she produced more stuff out of her lucky packet of a carrier-bag: nut trays fashioned from ice-cream lolly sticks, a doll-house lounge suite made out of beer cans, and painted glass discs.

Neighbour Clive almost fell off his stool in his eagerness to see what she'd conjure up next. A month earlier, he'd taken up a position next to me with his "*Snoere & Moere*". That's the way I translated the "Strings & Things" that meets my eye every day. A silver spoon, with no strings attached – they needn't worry about tomorrow.

Dalena and I did matric together; Clive went to another school. It seems like just the other day, though nearly two years have passed. Dalena's father has all the right contacts. She fell straight into a job with the Museum Council, or something. And Clive's old man is filthy rich, so he doesn't really have to work. My father is a salesman and he says just wait and see, what with affirmative action, he'll be out of a job one of these days. He says it nearly every evening. Just across from the flea market there's a man with a piece of cardboard hanging round his neck. His face and throat are red. The words written on the cardboard read: UNEMPLOYED, PLEASE HELP! He wears the same shirt and pants every day. It makes me shudder.

It is also thanks to Dalena's father that I got my stall. Now and then I sell one of my potty brooches. People are after odd things these days – not handmade brooches any more.

Browsing fever has the country in its grip. My cousin Rocco's article in last month's *De Kat* about different home industries was about just that. Yuppies in particular search tirelessly for new "conversation pieces". The latest collectors' craze is for naive art, and as one woman, pink-rinsed poodle under her arm, said at Clive's stall,

"Especially things made by real backvelders . . . Afrikaners. They're a dying breed, you know." She pointed at a set of handmade braces from the Great Depression. At any rate, that's what Clive assured her they were. Would she have a doll somewhere in her house, I wondered, like in Madame Tussaud's? One with Krisjan de Wet's hat and Jopie Fourie's shoes and – after today – Depression braces?

I could see how Clive sized up the treasures coming out of Dalena's goodies bag. As the two glasses stood brownly amongst my brooches, he started quizzing her. Clive and his old man often attend insolvency sales. I know because that's when I have to look after his stall.

Dalena loves hanging around the market during the lunch hour because she has her eye on Clive. "You'll never guess what, Jossie," she said. "Because then I landed up in this little dump, the hotel is closing down, wind mills wherever you look, pepper trees – that's all that'll grow there – whitewashed stones down the side of the streets, if you could call them streets, hey, one Saturday morning I buzzed down there with Toby – he's my boss, you know – we went to check out the restoration of some church. Renovation, you know. The loveliest windows . . . What was I saying?" Dalena never completes a sentence, she shunts off down another track until she gets back to where she was. "Anyway, the place is still ticking over – there are still sixteen townsfolk and the farmers round about – arch conservatives, kid, you should have seen how they checked me out, I was wearing this little top."

I looked at the two dark brown glasses with interest. The colour reminded me of beer bottles, I told Dalena.

"That's exactly what they are," she said in the tone of one who can no longer keep a secret to herself. "There's this old chap, you'd never believe it – a real museum piece – he sits there on the shop veranda at his little table, Jossie baby, and what does he have?" Dalena licked her lips. "Glass. Things made out of glass, and you know how mad people are about it at the moment. All sorts of things out of recycled glass. Most of it junk, you know, but I took a fancy to these glasses. Thought you'd like them." As she said this, she tucked back a curl and ogled Clive in the same movement.

"Toby asked him how he managed to fix the two halves together but he said that's his secret. Feel how sturdy . . ." and she thrust the cool brown glass with its slightly uneven form into my hand.

Dalena was still weaving between the other stalls on her journey back to the office when two people asked at almost the same time how much the glasses were.

"They're not for sale," I explained. "They're a gift from a friend."

Clive asked me to keep an eye on his things. He wanted to get a beer. He usually drank soft drinks. "Lend me your glasses," he said when he returned, and tried to work out how the old man had conjured two glasses out of one beer bottle. He shook his head. There was a missing link somewhere. A hole in the formula. And all the time I was thinking he wanted the glasses to pour me some beer.

I'd also like to know very much how you transform a common old beer bottle into two wine glasses.

The opportunity came sooner than I expected because Rocco was commissioned by a magazine to do a photo story on the "worst drought in living memory". He invited me to go along on the long ride.

We took pictures of despairing people in khaki or shabby blue overalls, busy off-loading bales of fodder from trucks to thin bleating sheep.

"Perhaps you'll bring us rain," said a man with lines deeply etched round his eyes. He pointed north where a few stray clouds lay before a colourless ridge. "The wind is right," said the farmer, gazing for a long time into my eyes, as though he saw the clouds reflected there.

The next day, the Saturday morning, we arrived at the small dorp where Dalena had found the glasses made from bottles. Rocco took a few shots of shops with boarded-up windows, lorries piled with fodder, dust devils in the veld, carcases.

It was the last Saturday of the month and the business street – the only tarred one – bore some signs of life. A couple of cars with unfamiliar registration plates stood before the hotel. The street market was just as Dalena had described it, like a church fête when almost everything's been sold. There were a couple of long tables, one or two folding stands and trestles with loose planks, here and there boxes stacked on top of one another, covered with an old sheet. The ginger beer looked even warmer in the oppressive weather, the home bakes ill at ease on the long empty tables. The people were more interesting than the merchandise. Their faces seemed to have become part of the landscape.

I found Oupa Moos just as Dalena had said, tucked away behind the shop wall, his hair as white as slaked lime. His table bore a couple of old-fashioned bottles, delicate ornaments, a stained-glass pane, and half a dozen dark brown wine glasses. We fell into conversation. His eyes, dim with age, had the expression of a listening child's. When I asked him, he said his sons were out of work; the farmers had reduced not only their flocks and herds, but also their helpers. He was paying for his grandson and granddaughters' education because their parents couldn't. When I said good-bye, he invited me to come and look around his workshop later that day.

That afternoon, I walked alongside houses ringed with white walls, past spiky cemetery cypresses, grey from continuous dust storms, through a *braksloot* and in between cottages with tiny rectangular gardens. Some houses were a pale blue or pale yellow. They reminded me of kindergarten art.

The cloud-bank looked increasingly threatening. I had to shield my eyes from the red dust that whirled up from the streets.

Oupa Moos's workshop was a thatched lean-to against the back of his house. It afforded him a little shade and a place to work. He was already busy melting some bottles. A primus stove hissed companionably. Round him lay or hung a variety of glass cutters and pliers; wire of varying thicknesses, stands and containers, and something like candle wax. Mirrors with name tags hung on the walls. It looked as though he was framing and decorating them.

He wore thick-lensed spectacles when he worked. I noticed he had to look very closely to see what he was doing. Every now and then I picked up the smell of singed hair, when he came too close to the flame. His face was red from the heat and tension, but it might also have been from pleasure. He wiped a newly-completed wine glass with a cloth and ran a finger over it to make sure that the edge was smooth.

Step by step he showed me how he heated the bottle and let it cool quickly; how the two halves fell apart perfectly; how he fused the neck of the top half to the base of the lower half; and how he then parted them at the neck, leaving each half with a small pedestal. Then he smoothed away the sharp edges.

"Here," he said when I was ready to leave. "I've got something special for you, Miss." He shuffled out ahead of me, into the dim house with the blue gingham curtains, shoo-ed off a few inquisitive children and came shuffling back out of the dark back room with something wrapped in brown paper.

He put it carefully on the workbench. When he opened the paper, there lay, on a bed of dark blue felt, between wooden wedges on a frame, eight rectangular pieces of glass, arranged from short to long. A carefully worked mallet accompanied them. He let the mallet dance over the glass. The sound was sweet and soothing.

"I can't accept this."

"Yes, you can, Miss. This is the first time anyone has taken such an interest in my work. It's not for sale," he said quickly when he saw me glance towards my bag.

I'd hardly made it back to the hotel when the weather broke. It started with wind tearing through the town. I heard sheets of corrugated iron groan, saw them crumple in the street. I watched the red curtain of dust close over the houses, and shortly after that I heard the plink plonk of drops on the iron roof. And then the rain came down. It seemed like hours that I lay on my bed listening to the claps of thunder, and the water and the wind and, later, the crashing hail.

By dusk it was over. People stood about, thunderstruck. The dull dusty colours were gone. Everything was focused and clear in the light of the setting sun. A police van was parked across the bottom of the road. Harsh blue light flashing. Red earth. I went to look at the swirling yellow water in the *braksloot*. It was a river now. The cypresses in the church yard were washed clean. Bright green spikes against the sky. But they'd been badly damaged by the storm; ripped foliage lay strewn about. The hailstones under the trees hadn't melted. Children skated down the street which was as slippery as a mirror.

Rocco's camera flashed; his face glowed. He spoke to a stubble-jawed man who leaned on his garden gate in a vest with slack braces, and a beer bottle in one hand, staring at the churning water and the distant lightning. Through the open door of the flat-roofed house I watched a stooped, black-clad woman take a blanket off the mirror in the passage. My pumpkins, the man told Rocco tersely. My pumpkins are buggered. Orange shards of pumpkin lay scattered about.

Oupa Moos! I rushed over to a police officer beside the van. He was talking on his two-way radio. I have to get through here, I said, kicking off my shoes. He shook his head. I had to wait. A few people were already waiting where the road disappeared under water.

On the other side of the *braksloot* – still a churning mass of water – I saw people putting up cardboard where there'd been window glass before; the shattered splinters gleamed in the last rays of the sun.

We waited for the water to subside. An icy wind was blowing by the time the constable allowed us to feel our way over the low-water bridge. Now that the storm water had rushed over it, the road to the *skema* with its red sandy soil looked like blood, the washed out limestone like bones.

Oupa Moos sat on a chair beside his front door. He seemed to be listening intently to the sound of drops from the broken gutter.

I knew then, I didn't have to ask. The hail had cut right through Oupa Moos's thatched lean-to as though every piece of ice was a laser beam.

Back at the hotel, I found Rocco in his element. "This kind of luck goes beyond any freelancer's wildest dreams. With this lot I can write my way onto the front page of every newspaper." I read over his shoulder on the screen of his laptop PC:

STORM BREAKS OUT OF HELL

"Isn't that a bit melodramatic?" I asked, although I wasn't sure any other words would really describe what had happened. Rocco worried at the blurb.

STORM FROM HELL BREAKS DROUGHT SUFFERING

"How can you say the suffering is over?"

He looked at me without comprehension. The screen reflected a flash of distant lightning.

> *From our special correspondent, M* – A drought, that according to locals has lasted seven years, was savagely broken yesterday afternoon when a devastating rain and hail storm struck the town and surrounds. On some farms in the district up to 75 mm fell in half an hour, and in the town, hailstones the size of golf balls wreaked havoc in vegetable gardens and orchards, when 68 mm was measured between 16h00 and 16h45. Telephone lines were damaged and the only contact with the outside world is . . .

Rocco read with me. He tut-tutted. "What other word can I use for 'devastation'? Come on, help. Quickly."

A family of four are thought to have drowned when the donkey cart they were riding on was carried off by a side stream of the Brak River.

"Shouldn't you begin by saying something about the people? And what about the suffering there on the other side of the *braksloot*?"

For the second time Rocco looked at me as though he didn't understand what I was saying, as though I was talking a foreign language. But more seriously – as if I was no more than a dim shadow behind a misted window pane.

I didn't really sleep. It was still dark when Rocco called me.

"We have to get going," he said. "I have to get to a fax machine."

"So you've missed the Sunday edition?"

"Yes. But I've adapted my story."

I packed without enthusiasm, placing the pieces of glass among my clothes. Then I had an inspiration, and I put the glass pieces back on to the frame. I drew the small mallet lightly over the glass keys.

But the sound was different – it didn't sound as it had the previous day. It sounded like drops of water against a window pane. *M. H.*

 Born in 1947 in Cradock, Eastern Cape, George Weideman completed his schooling in Springbok in Namaqualand. He began writing "seriously" at thirteen. His first collection of poetry, *Hondegaloppie*, was published in 1966, his latest, *Uit hierdie grys verblyf*, in 1987. He has also published two collections of prose (*Tuin van klip en vuur* and *Die donker melk van daeraad*). In 1992 he won the Sanlam Silver Prize for Youth Literature for *Los my uit, paloekas!*, and in 1994 *Die optog van die aftjoppers* garnered Gold. Before he took up a lecturing post at the Peninsula Technikon in Bellville, he taught at the University of Namibia in Windhoek; some of his works for theatre were performed at "Kampustoneel" by students of this university.

Miriam Tlali

A second look

Since completing my studies and entering the business world of the nineties – a highly competitive world in which trust and distrust often replace each other at lightning intervals – I have had more than enough reason to think back to a day when I was twelve years old.

As a little girl I had always loved and revered my five uncles, my mother's brothers. They seemed indestructible and fearless. And of all of them Malome Tšitso was to me the symbol of perfection. But there came a day when Nkhono, my beloved grandmother, made me pause to take a second look at those I trusted so completely.

To us grandchildren, Nkhono was not just "Nkhono". We all referred to her in possessive terms. She was "Nkhon'aka" – *my* grandmother, "Nkhon'aka" being the shortened form of "Nkhono oa ka". Each one of us had to emphasise that Nkhono belonged to us! Nkhono looked on my mother, Moleboheng, her only daughter, as her ally in the "sea" of males surrounding her. My grandfather was a domineering man, like his sons. He was from "Bakoena ba ha Lepitse", meaning "Those who have the crocodile as their totem animal". And he would always refer to members of his family as "Bakoena ba ha Lepitse, *maila-ho-ngoatheloa*" – those who cannot bear to be fed by others. He came from very proud patriarchal stock.

My mother's name, Moleboheng, means "Give thanks unto God" or "All mortals be thankful to Him, the Creator". Though she was pampered and admired by her father and the very apple of his eye, my mother, being the only other female around, became Nkhono's soul companion, one of her kind. "E ne e le ba *moloko* o le mong" – they were of the same *species* – for my mother understood what it was like to be a woman. She grew up to understand and feel the pain of being taken for granted, of being expected to bear burdens and suffer in silence, and to be at the service of others who very rarely appreciated it.

I was also a coddled one, but only because I was the youngest of my mother's three daughters. I was the baby, Ngoan'aofela. My childhood was in a sense a protracted one. With no one younger than myself around, my grandmother carried me on her back until I was old enough to go to school. A special bond grew between us. Having been widowed early in her marriage, my mother was the breadwinner. She was absent for long times, working in the homes of whites, and my elder sister, 'Mabaile, and I stayed at Nkhono's home.

The whole matter of closeness with our grandparents was to us grandchildren a very satisfactory and natural process. In the extended family, we were never quite able to distinguish to whom we really "belonged", spiritually or emotionally. And to me it was a time of trust in everybody belonging to this extended family.

But then a serious illness befell my beloved Nkhono. And during that illness something happened that made me grow up. The transition was traumatic, painful and abrupt.

While Nkhono was so ill, I would play a game of hopscotch on the verandah near her bedroom window in the afternoons, when everyone had gone back to work. Now and again, I would pause to go into the room to see whether she was comfortable. She had suffered a stroke, with the result that her speech had been impaired. But with time, she had recovered some fraction of it, and I was the only one who could decipher her seemingly incomprehensible mumblings and gestures. This particular afternoon, I could see that Nkhono had something very important to tell me because her eyes virtually shone as her tongue struggled with the words. When I entered the room for the third time, she beckoned me to come closer. She drawled along laboriously but I knew what she wanted. There was urgency in her voice and her sentences were precise and to the point. She signalled to me to raise her so that she could sit up a little. I was only twelve then, and I propped her up with all the strength my tender arms could muster. She rested on her weak elbow, mumbling and pointing instructions with her other arm, and ordered, "Koala lemati u le notlele!"

I moved fast to close the door and lock it as she had commanded. "Ntša senotlolo u bule lekase."

I alone knew where Nkhon'aka kept the key to her precious chest in the corner of the bedroom next to her bedstead. I took it out. I was shivering as my mind tried to figure out what was going to happen. As I prised open the heavy lid of the chest, the penetrating aroma of invisible mothballs hit my nostrils. Starched, snow-white sheets and pillowcases, layers of blankets, eiderdowns, dresses, skirts, blouses and other clothing lay in neat rows.

All the time obeying and responding to Nkono'aka's urgent gesticulations, I raised the lid of the separate small compartment on the left in which she kept her Bible, the baptismal certificates of all her children and some of her grandchildren, and other valuable documents. It was like entering an awe-inspiring sacred chamber. Below the stack of envelopes, lay Nkhon'aka's *nqele*, made of very soft leather, the top opening drawn tight with a woven-in leather string.

"Bula mokotlana oo u bale chelete eo!"

Summoning all my courage, I opened the money-bag and counted the wad of banknotes with trembling hands. I could feel the sweat building up on my brow. I had never seen that much money in my whole life.

"U tseba hore ke chelete e kae?"

I knew how much money it was and nodded, my trembling lips unable to compose a meaningful reply. It was several hundreds of rands. And at that time it was an incomprehensible treasure, especially to a child like myself who had never really been exposed to the realities of the world of material possessions, the very demanding means of accrual and the implications embodied in the whole process of the accumulation of wealth.

And then my grandmother asked me to do something I had never thought was possible. She indicated to me to remove one of the plump pillows which we children were never allowed to use, from under her head.

"Batla lehare u qhaqhe mosamo oo ka holimo!"

By now I was completely terrified. Why did I have to get a razor blade and open the top of that pillow? I did not know what the implications were of what Nkhon'aka was asking me to do. What had the money and the opening up of her best pillow, the one she had made from the tenderest, fluffiest goose-down – *masiba a ganse* – to do with each other? What was happening to my dear grandmother's mind anyway? Her serious illness had already inflicted suffering on my heart, now I tried hard to puzzle out through my fear whether she was losing her sanity. Nkhono was my whole life. And if she lost her mind, what would happen to me? As I cut the cotton threads one by one, my tears fell onto the pillow. She tried to comfort me. She patted my arm with her shaky hand and cried anxiously: "U se ke oa lla, Masolinyana!" – Please do not cry, Little-Teardrops.

She instructed me to take from under the bed one of her wash basins and to put some of the down in it. I did as I was told. When the pillow was only half full, she told me to take the *nqele* and put it in the middle, among the feathers. Then she gestured to me to replace the feathers from the basin and sew up the pillow again.

As I was sewing the top of the pillow, my grandmother mumbled along, her frail voice faltering as she gasped for breath in between disjointed sentences and phrases. She explained the reason for all her tiresome efforts, "Ha ke shoele mona, bo-Malom'ao ba tla fihla ba suthisa setopo sa ka ba batla chelete hohle ka tlung ka mona."

I cried loudly. Was my Nkhono really going to die? Why did she say that when she was dead, my uncles would put her corpse aside and search for her money all over the house?

Why should God take away the most precious gift He had given me? I looked into her eyes and into my heart, pleading with God never to take her away from me. I couldn't imagine myself living on this earth without Nkhon'aka. I wished my mother was there to stop God from taking her away. She must also have been thinking of her dear Moleboheng then because she made me swear that I would never disclose our secret to anyone but my mother when she arrived. In the midst of sweat, tears and drops from my running nostrils, I nodded again and again, unable to speak, but assuring her all the time that I would keep my promise.

And there in the midst of my grief, I suddenly realised the implication of her words – my revered uncles, my adored Malome Tšitso, searching the house for their mother's money? No!

I replaced the treasure-bearing pillow under Nkhono's head and she seemed to have found satisfaction at last. I locked the chest and hid the key where only she and I knew. But in that short time, I had ceased to be the "baby" I had been all my life. My Nkhono's illness had ushered me, very painfully, into the world of profound perplexities and the fear of the selfishness of others.

But my grandmother did not die. Not then. My mother did arrive a few days later to find her still alive. I was relieved when she finally came because before that I had the difficult task of keeping the secret truce with my grandmother – the first and only sacred concealment

136

I've held up to this day. My mother was the only one I had been instructed to divulge the secret to.

From that day on, I could not stop thinking of my grandmother's words whenever I looked at my uncles. It was when I stared searchingly into my Malome Tšitso's eyes that my heart really sank.

Ivy Compton-Burnett once said that time "is not a great healer. It is an indifferent and perfunctory one. Sometimes is does not heal at all. And sometimes when it seems to, no healing has been necessary." But it was time which came to my rescue and restored my faith in my beloved Malome Tšitso. When, years later, my grandmother lay on her deathbed and drew her last breath, it was the soothing hand of her ever-faithful, ever-caring son Tšitso that patted her eyelids and closed them. True to his name, which means "help" or "guidance", he had nursed her himself, day and night, not trusting anyone to attend to her needs. I was married by then and had had to leave Nkhono's home. But time, the kind healer of all wounds, had stepped in to reassure me that Malome Tšitso was the best son any mother could ever want to bring into this world of uncertainties.

 Born in Doornfontein, Johannesburg, Miriam Tlali grew up in Sophiatown. She attended St Cyprian's Anglican School and Madibane High. Financial difficulties forced her to abandon her studies at Wits University, and she went to work in a department store. *Muriel at Metropolitan* was based on her experiences there. She has served on the Committee of Women against Apartheid, was local editor for the U.S.-based literary magazine, *Straight-Ahead International*, and has recently been involved in the Women's National Coalition. Earlier on she participated in the International Writing Program at Iowa State University, was writer-in-residence at Ohio State University and a visiting scholar at Yale University. Most of her writing was banned in the apartheid years, and much of it has appeared in translation. After *Muriel* came *Amandla, Mihloti* and *Footprints in the Quag*, and *Crimen Injuria*, a play written and performed in Holland in 1984. She has regularly contributed to *Staffrider* magazine, of which she was co-founder.

Kaizer M. Nyatsumba

Streets of Hillbrow, here I come

I will never trust anyone again for as long as I live. Never.

I know you will probably not take me seriously, and dismiss me as an angry twelve-year-old who has yet to experience life. Just like my former parents did. But I tell you. I will never trust anybody again for as long as I live.

What experience do I still need to know that people are totally unreliable? If my own parents cannot be trusted, then who else can be? Experience! My foot, man.

As for my former parents, I would like to kill them. If I cannot do it myself, then I will have to get somebody to do it for me. The comrades, maybe. I know the comrades would not hesitate to do so. I only need to tell them the two were sell-outs.

Did I hear you shouting parricide? Parricide. What an ugly word that is! I cannot remember where I heard it, but it has stuck in my mind. Anyway, if you knew my former parents you would understand. You would have thought that as responsible parents they would think about me in the first place. Worry about my happiness, you know, like parents sometimes do on television. No, not those two. They were each so consumed by their own hatred for each other and by their secret passions that they forgot I existed. They never consulted me about the whole thing. Who was I to be consulted by them? After all, they are old, and experienced in life, aren't they?

Experience *se moer*, man! I do not care one hoot for their experience. I hate them. God knows I do. I wish they could be struck by lightning and die instantly. Then I would be truly without parents, and I would be able to forget them the next day. I mean it.

You see, although I have now decided to disown them and look upon them only as my former parents, and call them by their first names, I cannot help thinking about them at times. What's worse, I know they still consider *me* as *their* son, and probably even talk about me to those with whom they now live.

138

Begin to think of how they hurt me. The humiliation. More than any decent person can take. Last week, for instance. There I stood before this fat, ugly-looking white man dressed in black. The judge. He kept gawking at me over his spectacles, asking me stupid questions as I stood in what they called the "witness box". Boy, I shook like a reed, but he didn't notice.

And then there were the two bastards – my former parents, I mean – sitting at opposite ends of the room. Next to each one of them sat a black guy, also dressed in black. Their lawyers. I was the prize in this stupid competition with which I had nothing to do.

My former parents kept smiling at me whenever I looked their way. When I answered questions, they looked at me and listened attentively, each trying to get my attention. Taking me for a fool.

"Justice," my former father's lawyer said, "it is important that you tell this court the truth about your mother. Is it not true that she often scolds you at home?"

"Mister," I told him, shaking a little, "this has nothing to do with you."

"It happens to be a very important question, Justice. It will help this court reach a decision about which of your parents should be given custody of you. That means, which one you should live with. Now, please answer the question," he said.

"What question?"

"I asked you if it was not true that your mother always berates you at home."

"That she always *what*?"

"Berates you. Scolds you – that she likes to scold you."

"But so does my father next to you," I said, looking at my former father. He frowned, while my former mother smiled.

"Tell me, Justice," the lawyer went on, "do you like your mother?"

"No," I answered quickly. "I hate her. I hate her with all my life."

"I have no further questions. You . . ."

"But I would like to say that I also hate my father – equally strongly," I added.

I was not going to make it easy for them. They had each spoken to me before the court case, and told me to say bad things about the other one and choose them. They gave me money too – each one separately, of course. I said nothing then. I just looked at them. I was going to show them the real me in court.

My former mother's lawyer then stood up. He put his papers on the stand in front of him and glared at me.

"Justice, my boy . . ."

"I am *not* your boy!" I shouted.

The fat judge looked at me and frowned.

"Look, Justice," my mother's lawyer continued, "your mother loves you, you know that. She would like . . ."

"No, she does not love me. If she did, we would not be here today."

"Son, your mother . . ."

"Mister, I am *not* your son, and I never will be."

The judge adjusted the spectacles on his fat nose and stared at me.

As if I'd never spoken, the guy went on, "Is it not true, Justice, that your father is seeing another woman, and that that's why your parents are now divorcing?"

Divorce! That is another ugly word.

"Mister," I replied, as slowly as I could, "I don't know what you are talking about. I have not seen any woman."

And so it went. There was no question I answered simply. I always tried to evade them, just as I used to see people do in *L.A. Law* on television, and I said instead what *I* wanted to say.

Then it was the judge's turn. When he had finished scribbling something on the papers in front of him, he adjusted his spectacles again and looked straight at me. If he was trying to make me afraid, it did not work.

Judge: Justice, the facts presented to me indicate that your parents' marriage is irredeemable, and divorce will be granted. Will you please tell this court why your mother should not be given custody of you?

Me: Because I hate and despise her, Sir. That's why. I cannot live with someone I hate, can I now?

Judge: Would you like to live with your father, then?

Me: No, Sir. I hate and despise him, too. I hate both of them equally strongly and enough not to want to live with either of them.

Judge: Your parents are divorcing, young man, and you will have to be given into the care of either one of them, unless there are very

140

special reasons. I need not remind you that in terms of the South African Children's Act you are still a minor, and should therefore be cared for by your parents. Now, which of your parents would you like to live with?

Me: Neither, Sir.

Judge: Why not?

(Now, if there is anything I hate, it is being asked stupid questions.)

Me: Because, as I have already said, Sir, I would like to stay with *both* my parents, but the moment they separate they are no longer my parents and I will live with neither of them.

The judge scribbled something in his papers and asked no more questions. If the twitching of his fat nose was anything to go by, he was far from being pleased with me.

Not wanting to cooperate didn't help. In the end the judge pronounced my former parents, Siphiwe and Zanele Phalishi, legally divorced. And he said, peering over his spectacles at me, he could find no reason why he should not "award" me to Mrs Zanele Phalishi. He added something about my former father having unlimited visiting rights to see me, whatever that meant.

I came out of that court swearing. I was determined to embarrass my former parents. I swore louder whenever we came near people as we walked out of the court building. My former parents, walking on either side of me, however, looked happy. Even Siphiwe, though he had lost the battle for my custody. (Yes, I will call them by their first names.)

And so now here I am in Hillbrow with other children almost like me. I am learning many new things quite fast. Although this is only my third day here.

But that's me. I have always been quick to learn. I must admit it was not that easy at first. The public toilets are filthy, the empty buildings in which we sleep are cold and scary, the flattened cardbord boxes nothing like the old but warm and comfortable bed in my room at home. The first night, I almost gave up and returned home.

School? No, that is no longer for me. How could I continue going to school with children from normal families, while I no longer have parents? But I must admit, I still miss my friends in standard five. And I *wanted* to study. Let me tell you, I had hoped to be a medical doctor one day. But those two bastards have shattered my dream. I

141

know you will say they will finance my studies and that I can still become a doctor, but that is not good enough for me. Nothing will satisfy me as long as the two most important people in my life do not live together.

So, let my school friends and my teachers go on wondering what has happened to me.

I have found new friends.

I learn different things now. I am already beginning to master the crafts of pick-pocketing and begging for food and money. It is not as difficult as I thought it would be. Eyes round, mouth drooling and voice quivering, I approach people, paint for them the picture of a starving orphan who has nobody to look after him and ask for money, or food. Always for food, my new friends advised me when I first joined them.

But I haven't told you the whole story yet. Do you know what Zanele did when we got home from court last week? She threw Siphiwe's things out of the house. When Siphiwe came by lorry in the evening to fetch everything the court had awarded to him, our neighbours in Orlando East stood outside their homes and watched. And how they gossiped – right there in front of our house. It was a free show for all. I could not take it. Even Spinks's mother, Mrs Mazambane, was there, laughing with all the other people gathered in front of our house. She, whose husband beat her every weekend whenever he was drunk!

That same night the guy who had represented Zanele in court came to our home. He was no longer dressed in black. "Is Zanele in?" he asked when I opened the door.

So he was now calling her by her first name, and no longer Mrs Phalishi! I thought. I pushed the door shut and went back inside. When Zanele asked me who it was, I told her a thing or two. She knows me. She knows I don't mind giving her a piece of my mind, anytime.

She went to open the door for him and invited him in, in a voice I could hardly recognise. It was so soft, so sweet! They spent a long time in the bedroom, while I sat twisting my fingers in the lounge. The television set and video machine had been awarded to Siphiwe.

Then the man was there every night, and each time the two of them would spend hours in the bedroom. It seemed to me the man was just like the lawyers in *L.A. Law*, who spent more time in bedrooms than in courtrooms.

When they came out of the bedroom last Friday, Zanele was adjusting her skirt. In the kitchen she kissed him and, thinking I could not hear her from the lounge where I was sitting, said, "See you tomorrow, sweetheart. You are a good lawyer in court, but you are even better in bed."

And so that was what was going on. I disappeared the same night. Hillbrow is a far better place.

That house in Orlando East! We had our fair share of fun and happiness there. There were the times when the three of us sat together in the lounge, watching TV or hired videos, the days when, as a family and clad in our black and white Orlando Pirates tracksuits, we walked to Orlando Stadium down the road to watch the Buccaneers playing, the days when we attended music festivals at Shareworld or went to see movies in Johannesburg. We were happy then, and Zanele and Siphiwe called each other "sweetheart" and "lovie". Those were my parents. Those are the days I would like to remember.

There were also times when my parents quarrelled and did not talk to each other. Those days were few, though. Whenever Zanele and Siphiwe quarrelled, they always made up and we were all happy again. Those were my parents.

But two years ago really angry quarrels started taking place. They would fight every week. And that was when I heard the word "divorce" mentioned in my family for the first time. It was when I was in my room preparing to sleep, one night. I had finished saying my prayers when I heard them shouting at each other in their room. I listened. I was worried because they had never shouted at each other that way before.

I knelt on my bed and prayed again. I asked the Lord to grant happiness to my parents and make them stop arguing, I prayed for peace in the family. But my mother's shrill voice cut through my prayers.

"... don't think that I am dependent on you. I have my own qualifications, you know. I can make it on my own," she shouted.

"You keep talking about these *impressive* qualifications of yours ever since you got that B.A. degree from Vista University. What is a B.A. these days, especially from a bush college with no academic standards?"

"Don't think because you studied at UCT and have a Master's degree, you're so unique. Stop boasting about it as if you're the only man in this country holding an M.A. from UCT, that pale, male, English liberal laager."

"Let's talk about something else, shall we?"

"Like what, Siphiwe? Like what?"

My father did not answer. My mother then dropped the bombshell.

"I want a divorce, Siphiwe."

"You what?"

"You heard me. I want a divorce."

"What? Are you mad?"

"Don't think that just because *you're* mad all of us are. I mean it, I cannot live with a pompous pig like you any longer. My fourteen years . . ."

"Zanele, don't say things for which . . ."

"... with you were one long hell. I want to be free now."

"What about our child, eh? What about Justice – did you think about him?"

I did not hear her answer. I could not take it any longer, so I burst into their bedroom. They were embarrassed.

"Justice. I thought you were asleep," she said, her eyes wide.

"How can I sleep when the two of you are fighting in here? What is going on?"

My father looked at my mother. My mother looked at my father. Neither replied. Dad put his hand on my shoulder and said, "Go to bed, son. I will talk to you tomorrow morning."

Tomorrow came and went. Nobody told me anything. They would not even talk to each other – for weeks. Then my father started to come home late from work. My mother soon did the same.

And then, like she said she would, my mother filed for divorce.

I tried to talk to them, but nobody listened to me. They each wanted what they wanted, and it did not matter one jot how I felt.

The case dragged on for almost two years, with them living under the same roof but sleeping in separate rooms. It was awful. I kept hoping it was a nightmare, and that I would wake up one day to find it wasn't true. Nothing of the sort happened.

Instead, I ended up in the witness box last week. How could I choose between two people I loved equally? The two most important people in my life?

There you are. I have told you the whole story. But I have no faith in this world controlled by adults. Adults with experience who understand *nothing*.

Streets of Hillbrow, here I am.

Kaizer Mabhilidi Nyatsumba is a political correspondent for *The Star* in Johannesburg. Born at White River in the Eastern Transvaal, he was educated at Dlangezwa High School, the University of Zululand, Georgetown University and the Newspaper Institute of America in Washington, D.C. He has published a book of short stories, *A Vision of Paradise*, and one of poetry, *When Darkness Falls*. He is a regular political commentator on Radio Metro.

Riana Scheepers

Garden-gate green, privy-pink, back-door blue

My mother came back from the dead. Two years after my father died, my mother started living again.

Late one afternoon, two men came to tell me and my mother that my father was dead. There'd been an accident in the mine where he worked. My mother first phoned my gran and grandpa, and then went to lie on her bed with a cloth over her eyes. She lay there for a very long time. As though she was dead too.

The next few days a lot of people came to our house. People I'd never seen in our town before. They came to call with pots of soup and boxes of biscuits and bunches of the lilies that grow wild here in Natal. They exchanged a few words with my mother in the dark room, then left again, shaking their heads as they went out into the street.

I longed for my father, and I couldn't understand why he'd gone away so suddenly and so frighteningly. Every evening I used to wait at the green gate for him to come home. When he saw me, he would wave to me, and then I'd run to meet him. He'd swing me up onto his shoulders and carry me home. "Ma, where are you?" he always called out just as we got to the house.

"Coming," she'd answer – usually from somewhere in the garden.

We always went to the pantry first. He'd pour us each a glass of ginger beer. The ginger beer was in a big brown crock that stood ready for us in the cool dimness of the pantry. Sometimes there were prickly pears in the milking bucket. He'd picked them the day before, and now he'd prepare them for us. Or peel a couple of oranges. And when my mother came in from the garden, he'd kiss her and pour her a glass of ginger beer too. Or give her a peeled prickly pear. Or an orange.

Then suddenly he didn't come anymore. Even though I still waited at the gate in the evenings.

I missed my mother too. Although she was in the house, I couldn't

146

get through to her. She lay on her bed in the dark with a wet cloth on her head. My gran came to fetch me and said that I must be very brave, I was almost grown-up, I was to stay with them for a bit until it was all over.

"What will be over?" I asked, but my gran didn't answer. I didn't want to stay with my gran and grandpa. Their house was full of strange pictures of angels that frightened me and the rooms smelt musty. At night I could hear my grandpa snoring right through the walls.

I wanted to be with my mother. I wanted her to hold me close and comfort me. But she couldn't. She just lay there, without crying, without talking, without even knowing I was nearby.

After a long time my mother got up and went back to work. But she wasn't alive. My pretty, pretty green-eyed mother was grieving and she wore long ugly dresses so she looked old and peculiar.

I came home again, slept in my own bed, went back to school, trained for athletics, but everything had changed. At night I'd wake up and hear my mother walking about the house. Like a ghost. At first her night walking frightened me. I thought it was burglars. But eventually even that didn't worry me.

I longed for my father, but I couldn't tell her.

I longed for my mother too. But how can you tell someone you miss them when you're with them?

A short time after my mother stopped wearing black dresses, a man started showing up at our house. A stupid man. An ugly man who came to the door all dressed up with his hair slicked down, carrying a ridiculous bunch of pink-dyed shop flowers. I had to open the door and say to him, come inside, my mother won't be long, would you like to sit down? And then I took his revolting flowers into the kitchen and stuck them into an empty jar. Often I'd just throw them straight into the rubbish bin, pink ribbon and all. My mother didn't notice at first. Or perhaps she did, but she didn't say anything. She never asked.

When he came round too often for my liking with his horrible shiny shoes and his "How's it going today with the blossom of my life?" I decided I wouldn't leave them alone together for a minute. When he arrived, I'd open the door and let him in without any greeting. I'd keep my eyes fixed on him, never looking away once. Although I knew I looked ugly. When my mother came in, I didn't leave. Not even if she asked me to make tea. I didn't answer, I didn't move, I simply sat and stared at him. Or I positioned myself beside my mother on the couch and pressed my head against her arm. No matter how long he sat there, I stayed. No matter whether I had homework or not, I sat there. He wasn't very pleased, I could tell, because when my mother wasn't looking or left the living room for a minute, he glared at me. But he didn't scare me. I didn't like him, and I wanted him to know it.

After a time he stopped calling.

But then there was another one. Another dumb thing with a red face and hairs poking from his nostrils. Who had the cheek to ask me, "Do you want a daddy again?"

"No," I said, giving him my look.

"But who's going to look after your mummy?" asked turkey-face.

"I am."

"Is that so?" He pulled his mouth into an ugly slit.

"Yes." I pulled my mouth into the same line as his.

After a while he stopped calling too.

But that was all long ago. The couple of men in the town who came courting my mother, thinking they might be able to marry her, soon realised they weren't welcome. I don't know whether it was my stares, but after a while they preferred to stay away.

Fine, I thought.

But the day my mother tidied the pantry, everything changed. It was a holiday, shortly after the beginning of summer, and it was raining. My mother always liked the rain. So did I. Especially when it came down so softly that you knew: we're in for a three-day drizzle.

"Today we're going to tackle the pantry," she said unexpectedly.

So we set to work. She took the door off and stood it in the passage to give her more elbow room. And then she took down the shabby scrap of curtain and gave it to me to throw in the bin, and then she pushed open the rusty window to let in great gulps of fresh air.

She tackled the shelves, clearing everything off them. All the empty preserving jars, the loose lids and rubber rings, the weevilly Tupperware containers, the half empty bags of ginger and coriander seeds, a packet of salt that was punctured and left a long white line when she moved it, a never-opened bottle of Buttalene, cans of meatballs in tomato sauce, opened condensed milk full of ants, a sheaf of old recipes the mice had got into, everything. Everything. Even the empty ginger beer crock. First she stacked everything on the kitchen table, then threw out the contents of the Tupperware and put the containers in the sink. She washed and rinsed the crock carefully and set it to one side. The rest of the pile she simply threw into the bin. It overflowed and I had to fetch Checkers bags and gather the spill into them.

Then my mother took a mop and a scrubbing brush, a bucket of warm soapy water, and Handy Andy and Mister Min, and started cleaning. From top to bottom she scrubbed the shelves, the window, the walls, the floor. I sat and watched from the kitchen. It was a wonderful sight.

"Right," she said every now and then as she worked. When it was all spick and span and smelling of Jik and Mister Min, we went out to the garage in the rain. We scratched about among my father's tools for a screwdriver to tighten the loose screws on the shelves. The one in the house wasn't up to the job.

I could tell from my mother's face that out there in the garage among my father's things, she was thinking of him and missing him. But she didn't start crying again. She had a brainwave.

"There's a whole lot of paint. What do you think? Shall we paint the pantry?"

"Yes. Good idea," I said.

"As soon as the walls are dry, we'll get going."

We returned laden with paint tins. The smudges on the rims showed us what colour was inside. I recognised them. It was the paint my father had used for the garden gate. And the back door. And the privy.

My mother prised open the lids with the screw driver. "You stir them," she said, passing me a short stick. "I'll get the brushes."

I helped my mother. We painted out our pantry with all the leftover paints. The ceiling and one wall were back-door-blue. The two side walls and all the shelves were privy-pink. The other wall and the door were garden-gate-green. It looked very funny, but nice.

"Right," said my mother, as we admired our new pantry, both of us tired and spattered with paint. "Now we can get on with our lives again. This very evening I'll make us some ginger beer."   C. K.

Born in 1957 in Natal, Riana Scheepers obtained an M.A. in Afrikaans and Dutch at the University of the Free State. While lecturing at the University of Zululand, her first book of short stories, *Die ding in die vuur*, received the ATKV Prose Prize. From 1990 to 1994 she lectured in the Department of Afrikaans/Nederlands at University of Cape Town, and is now with Tafelberg Publishers. Her *Dulle Griet* won the Eugène Marais Prize in 1991. Another two books of short stories appeared in 1994: *'n Huis met drie en 'n half stories* and *Haai Katriena, wat vertel jy my nou?* She is currently working on a Ph.D. on the work of Koos Prinsloo, a contemporary Afrikaans short story writer.

Word list

JENNY HOBBS – Two fishermen
amatungulu – *Carissa macrocarpa* – thorny sub-tropical shrub with glossy dark green
leaves and edible bright red fruit, also called Natal plum

PATRICK WALDO DAVIDS – Wings for Bulbie
bras – "brothers", friends
babalaas – hangover, here used as an adjective
dominee – minister of religion or clergyman in a Reformed church
laaitie – here: son
riempiesbank – bench with seat made of strips of animal hide
stoep – verandah
toppies – older men (informal)

SANDILE MEMELA – A life besieged
comrades – radical youths, friends/colleagues in the liberation struggle
DET – Department of Education and Training (that administrated black education)

HEIN WILLEMSE – A dark girl in Tepotzlán
Aqui estacionado Maria – literally: Here parks Mary
flor de clabaza – tortilla with vegetable filling
graffiti – scribblings or drawings, often indecent, found on public buildings
huitlacoche – (tortilla) filling made of the indigenous Mexican fungus that grows on
maize
La Morenita – The Dark One
mariachis – strolling musicians playing Mexican dance music
samosa – small, fried pastry triangle stuffed with curried meat or vegetables
tortilla – round, flat Mexican cake of wheat or maize, usually eaten hot with a filling
zocálo – public square

LINDSAY KING – A garbage story
blerry – bloody
larnies – here: employers
kwaai – here: persistent and sharp-tongued
enchie – cigarette
Wat's gemors in Engels? – What's rubbish in English?

JOHNNY MASILELA – Baba Mfundisi the clergyman
baba – term of respect, somewhere between father and Mr
bakkie – small truck
mfundisi – clergyman

DIANNE CASE – The crossing
bakkies – small trucks
mos – an untranslatable word, usually for emphasis, e.g. Ek het jou mos gesê – I told you, didn't I?
jy weet – you know
skollies – hooligans
wat te besig is om vir my te kom kyk – who is too busy to visit me

MARITA VAN DER VYVER – St Christopher on the Parade
Sy's swaar, nè? Wil jy dalk 'n lemoen hê? – She's heavy, isn't she? Do you perhaps want an orange?
UCT – University of Cape Town

LESLEY BEAKE – The new beginning
DP – Democratic Party
toppie – older man (informal)

LAWRENCE BRANSBY – A reflection of self
doek – headscarf

BARRIE HOUGH – The journey
imbongi – praise singer
skrik – fright
Suka! – Go away!

DIANNE HOFMEYR – The magic man
doek – headscarf

ENGELA VAN ROOYEN – Your own two hands
Abantu abadala ngama xoki – The old people are liars
ewe – yes
mtika – traditional long leather cloak
ubuntu – solidarity, support for one another, brotherhood of man

ZULFAH OTTO-SALLIES – A better life for you, Mums
breyani – Cape Malay rice dish with red meat, chicken or fish
Daa' eindig allie ouens wat met drugs sukkel – There all the guys end up that mess around with drugs
Dis sieke ma' (dis seker maar) onse geluk – That's just our luck